Jimmy Bench-Press

Also by Charlie Stella

Eddie's World

Jimmy Bench-Press

Charlie Stella

CARROLL & GRAF PUBLISHERS
NEW YORK

JIMMY BENCH-PRESS

Carroll & Graf Publishers
An Imprint of Avalon Publishing Group Inc.
161 William St., 16th Floor
New York, NY 10038

First Carroll & Graf edition 2002

Interior design by Simon M. Sullivan

All of the characters in this book are fictitious, and any resemblance to
actual persons, living or dead, is purely coincidental.

Library of Congress Cataloging-in-Publication Data is available.

ISBN: 0-7867-1057-8

Printed in the United States of America
Distributed by Publishers Group West

*This book is dedicated to the best thing that ever happened to me,
my beautiful wife, Ann Marie Stella.*

*Others I need to acknowledge for their help, support, and invaluable
advice, include my agent, Bob Diforio; my editor, Peter Skutches; Ann
Marie, and always, Dave Gresham . . . and the latest Bichon-Friese to
sign up, Gilda's co-star, Rigoletto.*

Life is often times stranger than fiction. When a corporation the size of Enron can implode at the expense of so many of its loyal employee-shareholders, leaving them without a job and/or retirement funds, after those overseeing the fiasco had already cashed out, one has to wonder if the term "organized crime" deserves a more inclusive definition.

Many elected officials received Enron political contributions on both sides of the political fence—the tribute paid up?

Enron's financial auditors, Arthur Andersen, shredded potentially incriminating documents—much the same way a bookmaker might shred betting slips?

The highest ranking Enron officials encouraged employees to buy as much Enron stock as they could, when the same officials already knew that Enron's value wasn't what the cooked books led to believe—"pump and dump"?

Organized crime doesn't always involve men with Italian names. Sometimes, probably more often than we'll ever know, it involves some of the most respected and accepted business people of our time. The double standard for corporate organized crime is grossly hypocritical. We all know what needs to be done with these Enron clowns should they ever be brought to justice and found guilty.

Instead of the federal country club circuit of prisons reserved for "respectable businessmen" who've lost their way, let them tour the real joints where we send all the other criminals of the so-called organized crime world.

A me, Faust!
(Come, Faust, with me)
—*Mephistofele*

Jimmy Bench-Press

Chapter 1

"How silly is this shit?" Jimmy Pinto said as he glanced at the piece of paper in his right hand.

It was eight-thirty in the morning. The sky was gray. The streets were still wet from a heavy rain that had just ended.

Jimmy Mangino sipped coffee from a Styrofoam Dunkin' Donuts cup as he scanned a row of attached brick two-family houses on Coyle Street opposite Sheepshead Bay High School. Mangino was a large muscular man in his mid-thirties. He had dark curly hair and thick eyebrows. Two days of beard stubble covered his face.

"How much money he give the barber?" Mangino asked.

Pinto was also a stocky man. He looked younger than his fifty-one years. He looked up from the piece of paper he was holding and waved it a few times. "Fifty-eight thousand," he said. "If you can believe it."

Mangino smirked. "These fuckin' jerkoffs," he said as he took another sip of coffee. "Money guys, they got nothing better to do."

Pinto bit his lower lip. "And us two standing out here like a pair of morons trying to collect it for them."

"There a chance this guy the barber has anything?" Mangino asked. He finished the coffee and was looking for a place to toss the empty cup.

"Probably not," Pinto said. "The guy didn't even own the joint where he worked cutting hair. The story is he got himself a Puerto Rican girlfriend, invested in her restaurant, the first ten thousand, after which he took a bath for his trouble."

"You mean your friend Larry took the bath," Mangino said.

"That's the story," Pinto said. He lit a Camel and took a long drag on the cigarette. "He's a zip. Sixty-two years old, off the fuckin boat, and he's supposed to be mortgaged up the ass. That house over there." He glanced back down at the paper. "Twenty-one, eighty-six."

"So it be like taking blood from a stone," Mangino said. "Trying to get fifty-eight large from him."

"Which is why Larry puts up a fifty percent fee on the collection," Pinto said. "He knows he's not seeing a dime of that money. He figures he'll get two jerkoffs, you and me in this case, to give the guy stiffed him some shit, maybe break him up a little. It's mean is all it is, having you and me here. He's pissed at himself because he did something stupid one more time in his ignorant fucking life, and now he wants the old man to pay for it."

Mangino lit his own cigarette, a Marlboro. He spoke with the cigarette in his mouth. "Except the guy did take the money and never paid it back," he said.

Pinto took a deep breath. "Would you give a barber don't own the shop he's working at fifty-eight large, Jimmy? Think about it."

"No fuckin way," Mangino said.

"Not that I'd have it to give, but no fuckin way is right," Pinto said. "Even you're dumb enough to start the guy with ten large, which is what stupid Larry did, that don't mean you go another forty-eight for Christ sakes. And that's what he did. He put up another forty-eight thousand. I guess to protect his initial investment, what he must've been thinking. Who knows. It seems like a better idea to go get it from Larry, though, the fifty-eight K. Or another fifty-eight K. Since the moron is so anxious to give out his money. You see what I'm saying?"

Mangino was eyeing a thick woman in a robe and slippers putting out her garbage across the street.

"I guess I'm just getting too old for this shit," Pinto said. "Playin' these games on my day off. For a rich moron needs to feel like a knock-around guy so he gives out fifty-eight thousand to a sixty-year-old zip with a thirty-year-old girlfriend. I tell you that, the broad he got the money for, this barber, she's thirty years younger than the old man?"

"Don't make him a bad person," Mangino said.

"Except he gave her up, the old man," Pinto said. "What Larry told me the old man said when he first went to see them for the money past due. The old man said to go get it from her, she's the one used it."

Mangino smirked again. "And I went away for being stupid," he said.

A light drizzle started to fall. Pinto opened his arms.

Mangino took a drag on his cigarette, glanced back at the row of houses and said, "We gonna stand out here much longer? I need to go see a paying customer this afternoon and I want to catch some of the Knicks game later."

"You still playing?" Pinto asked.

Mangino rubbed at his temples with his thumbs. "Why I gotta go see the paying customer," he said.

"I called, how many times so far? Three, right?"

"At least three."

"And all I get is the wife answers, tells me, Vittorio is asleep, she can't wake him."

"What he tells her to say, yeah."

"And she's gone now, how long, fifteen minutes about?"

"At least that. And there's no way he'll answer the phone."

"So we're getting nowhere fast."

"Except it's killing time I can't afford to lose right now," Mangino said. "And I can feel a headache coming on."

"Right, so fuck it," Pinto said. He stuffed the piece of paper inside his front pants pocket and turned toward the car parked at the curb.

The thick woman across the street was pushing a folded pizza box into one of the cans. Mangino, disgusted at the sight of the slippers she was wearing, made a face. He glanced around to see if anyone was watching, then dropped the empty coffee cup in the curb. Both men sat inside the black Buick LeSabre and immediately let their windows down a crack.

"Can I drop you anywhere?" Pinto asked Mangino. "Where's your pickup?"

"The Brooklyn Inn," Mangino said. "Sometimes the guy is short, he has one of his broads there blow me."

Pinto smiled. "A Sunday morning blow job," he said. "I could get used to that."

"Yeah," Mangino said. "It beats standin' around in the rain."

When Detective John DeNafria saw the car pull away from the curb on Avenue T, he closed the blinds. He had been watching the two men from the second floor bedroom window of Vittorio Tangorra's two-family house. DeNafria was a muscular man of average height and weight. He had dark hair and a short mustache. His skin was still tan from a recent trip to Puerto Rico.

The old man sitting in the armchair pointed at the window. "Who were they?" Vittorio Tangorra asked. He had just turned sixty-three years old. He was a frail man with receding white hair. He spoke with the remnants of his native Italian accent.

DeNafria turned away from the window and pulled a notepad from his back pocket. "Goons," he said. "Especially the bigger one. How often they come around?"

"This was the first time, those two," the old man said. "Larry and another one come around before. A couple of times, last month. Two weeks ago."

DeNafria wrote in his notepad. "That's when Larry hit you?" he asked as he looked up from the notepad.

"He smack me like child," the old man said. "Then he throw me down on the sidewalk outside. In front of my house."

DeNafria looked around the room they were in. It was mostly old furniture but well kept. Thick plastic wrapped the cushions of the armchair Vittorio Tangorra was sitting in.

"And they threatened your wife?" DeNafria asked. "Larry did?"

The old man pointed at a telephone on one of the night tables. "On the telephone," he said. "Once a week. Every couple of days."

DeNafria made a note of it. "Your wife is at church now, right?"

"She go to pray, yes," the old man said.

"What about the woman, Lucia Gonzalez?"

"That was a mistake."

"I understand. Where can I reach her?"

"She live in Jersey. North Bergen. She's Cuban."

DeNafria wet his lips. "You borrowed the money for her, right?"

The old man rubbed his forehead. "I make big mistake," he said. "I use most of my own money, too." He waved the next thought off.

"I'm going to want you to talk to Larry," DeNafria said. "I'll set up the telephone machine but I'm going to want you to get Larry to talk about this over the telephone, alright?"

"I don't have the money," the old man said.

"And Larry brought in a heavyweight," DeNafria said. "The one guy today, the big one, he's not going to care about your age."

The old man looked up. "You know him?"

"Jimmy Bench-Press," DeNafria said.

"Jimmy what?" the old man asked.

"He's a mean guy," DeNafria said. "I'll set up your telephone with the recorder and get going, alright?"

The old man shrugged. "Sure," he said. "What am I gonna do?"

DeNafria frowned. "Right," he said. "Exactly."

Chapter 2

Later the same morning, Jimmy Mangino sat with Eugene Tranchatta as they watched a homemade porno film in the manager's office of the Brooklyn Inn hotel.

The office was fairly large, with three desks, one behind the other, against one wall; a row of folding chairs lined against the opposite wall; and a small couch in the back. Tranchatta sat behind the last desk smoking a joint. A nineteen-inch television on a portable stand had been moved to the middle of the aisle to the right of the last desk. Mangino watched the television from the couch.

Tranchatta was a tall middle-aged man with big ears and a skin condition. He scratched behind his ears as he watched the video.

"She's not bad," Mangino said. He was watching a short woman with long dark hair giving head to a teenage boy wearing a football jersey.

"Janice Gottlieb," Tranchatta said. "Thirty-eight years old. Lives out in Suffolk somewhere. Holtsville, I think. Where the IRS is. She works the high school cafeteria dishing out lunches. By day a school mom, by weekends a homemade porn star. I'm tellin' you, Jimmy, this home porn shit has a nice market."

"But not nice enough you don't have to short me," Mangino said.

Tranchatta waved Mangino off. "Please," he said. "You love coming here to get head. What was it, two years you just did? I'd think you want me short more often than not after two years in the joint."

"I got all the head I wanted inside," Mangino said. He was still watching the film.

Tranchatta made a face. "Please," he said. "I just ate."

The woman in the film was suddenly on a queen-size bed. A second teenage boy joined the scene. The first boy straddled the woman's head from behind her. The other boy ducked his head down between her legs.

Mangino looked away from the television. "So tell me some more about this thing you got going," he said.

"What, with the movies?" Tranchatta asked. He set the remnants of the joint in an ashtray and lit a fresh Camel cigarette. "It started with this couple from Massapequa," he said. "Swingers they call themselves. Fuckin nuts, you ask me. They contacted me here one day. Out of the fuckin blue. They showed one night together, two couples. One guy owns a gas station out on Long Island somewhere and the other guy works for him fixing cars or some shit."

Tranchatta stopped to take another drag from his cigarette. "They had this private orgy, both couples, the guys fucking each others' wives, and they asked me to film it for them. A pack of nuts, right? Then they start bringing the wives with different guys. Very different guys, you know what I mean. A pair of Mandingos, for one thing. Black as the ace of spades. Hung like horses. Then they brought young ones. College kids. Maybe high school for all I know. I didn't card them. Then some guys looked like freaks. Huge guys, bodybuilders. Bigger 'n you, Jimmy.

Fucking humongous. All the time, these two mamalukes are watching the action right along with me while I'm filming it. This was all about two-three months ago. Then the last month they start showing up with other broads, too. The broad in the film there with the two college boys is one. Those guys have been here before with these guys' wives."

He took another drag on the cigarette. "The guy running the show claims they meet these people on the Internet. I don't know where he finds these nuts but he does. And now sometimes they show up, rent two-three rooms together and have a fuck fest. They even help me film it when they have a lot of action going on at once, they want different angles. Actually, they got me into it, the filming thing. I got cameras of my own now, even at the apartment where I live. I caught my landlord's daughter giving her boyfriend a hand job a couple times outside my door, you can believe it."

Tranchatta stopped to wipe his nose. He used a handkerchief that was stuffed in his back pants pocket. The handkerchief was spotted with blood.

"Anyway," he continued, "it's like this secret society these nuts have, but I'll tell you what, the psycho husband shows up here with cash every time. Greases the wheels like a champ and who am I to argue with that kind of thing? Nobody, right, so I don't. I take what they give me. And you know, they know I'm makin' copies of this shit. Which I think just turns these freaks on all the more, knowing it's out there. And the bottom line is, it keeps me from borrowing more money from guys like you. You notice I'm not looking for money lately, right?"

Mangino was rubbing his temples. "That's all very interesting," he said, "what didn't make me dizzy. But I meant the other thing. The real money." He touched the tip of his nose with a finger. "This stuff."

Tranchatta smiled. "Oh, that," he said. He stopped the VCR and turned in his chair to face Mangino. "Now that," he said, "is a beautiful thing."

"I'm listening," Mangino said.

Tranchatta set the Camel down in the ashtray and exchanged it for the joint. He used a clip to hold the tiny marijuana cigarette. He lit the tip of the joint with his lighter as he tilted his face to the left. He closed his right eye to the flame. He took a long drag on the joint. He set it back down in the ashtray and sucked in air before eventually letting the smoke escape his lungs.

Mangino continued to rub his temples. He was glaring at Tranchatta.

"I call it the noodle connection," Tranchatta finally explained. "Koreans, of all things. The same ones own the delis. I broker a move between the Koreans and this Russian dude, Vladimir. Dig the name, Vladimir. I call him Vladi for short. And he's not in the Russian mob. What he is, now get this, he's a fuckin waiter. A waiter over in Canarsie someplace. What the guy does, he moves the junk to a very discreet clientele and I'm his broker. I get, like, a grand or two every time they move more than a quarter pound. Which is more and more often lately. Two times a month lately. And there's another thing going on end of this week. Maybe Friday-Saturday afternoon, if you're free."

"And you just told me because why?" Mangino said. He was rubbing his forehead with two fingers.

Tranchatta shrugged. "Protection, man," he said. "I figure we can work something out. You just got out and I'm no tough guy.

Sooner or later, let's face it, somebody is gonna notice it, I'm no tough guy."

Mangino lit a cigarette. "And how much you figure protection is worth?" he asked.

Tranchatta reached for his cigarette, changed his mind and crushed it out as he shrugged again. "Being there's nobody on this planet I know of will ever fuck with you . . . What? Say sixty-forty on the noodle connection? Aside from any extra we find along the way. How's that, forty percent, your end, of whatever I broker?"

"If that's all there is to it," Mangino said. "If you're not leaving anything out. I can protect you for forty percent, sure."

"Then it's a deal," Tranchatta said. He picked up what was left of the joint he had been smoking, made a face, and set it back down. He lit a fresh Camel instead. He took a long drag on the cigarette, exhaled through his mouth, and looked directly at Mangino through the smoke. "Now," he said. "You want to see what I've got this morning. There's only about three girls working the Lounge from last night but any one of 'em can drain your hose like a wet-vac the porters use to dry up basement floods."

"I think I rather have the money today," Mangino said. "That okay with you?"

Tranchatta was surprised. He reached into his back pocket for his wallet and quickly pulled out three fifty-dollar bills. "One-fifty," he said. "All brand fucking new, too."

Mangino eyeballed his new partner. "If we're gonna work together, I'd like to keep things on a business level from now on."

Tranchatta looked from left to right and shrugged. He was suddenly nervous. "Sure, Jimmy," he said. "Whatever you say."

Mangino was off the couch. He took the three crisp fifty-dollar bills from Tranchatta and winked. "See you the weekend," he said.

A few hours after attaching the recorder to the old man's telephone in Brooklyn, Detective John DeNafria picked up Detective Alex Pavlik on his way through Manhattan to New Jersey. It was early in the afternoon. The sky had cleared just enough to filter sunlight through the thinning clouds.

Pavlik had just spent most of his morning working out in a gym on Forty-second Street. He was a tall broad man with bad knuckles from several years of both amateur and professional boxing. He had a deep voice and he took his time when speaking. Pavlik was dressed in heavy blue sweatpants and a gold zip-up sweat jacket.

"I guess this is welcome," DeNafria said.

"Thanks," Pavlik said.

The two men exchanged handshakes. DeNafria drove west on Forty-second Street. "You're the guy busted Timothy Waller, right?" he asked.

Pavlik nodded.

"That must've felt good, taking that psycho off the street."

"It almost got me fired," Pavlik said with a smirk, "nailing that piece of shit."

"All I'm hearing is gold shield."

"They figure it makes for better press if I'm a hero. That's what I've been told, more or less."

"Well, congratulations anyway. And trust me, the shield is a lot better than a criminal trial. You want to avoid those at all costs, let me tell you."

"You're talking about that Eastern Parkway thing, right?" Pavlik asked.

"I guess they filled both of us in, huh?" DeNafria said.

"I remember your situation. They had the damn thing on camera. I never understood why they put you through the ringer on that one."

"Tell me about it," DeNafria said. He veered around a UPS truck blocking the left lane. "Wrong cop in the wrong place at the wrong time," he continued. "It was in the middle of that other thing with those bozos with the nightstick. The blacks wanted blood. Some kid went to rob a guy at an ATM, I happened to be across the street and tried to stop it. The kid shot at me, more than once, and I fired back. The troublemakers tried to claim the shots the ATM camera caught the kid taking were warning shots. He wasn't really trying to kill me. I was lucky he hit the gym bag I was carrying. I fired back and nailed him. Next thing I know, I'm up on charges, my name's all over the paper and my wife is wondering why the fuck she married me. It's a lot of stress going through a trial that might land you in jail for doing your job. I don't recommend it."

Both men were quiet a few minutes. Pavlik broke the silence. "Well, at least you're looking tan," he said. "Where'd you go?"

"Puerto Rico," DeNafria said. "Alone. My marital problems only got worse after the trial."

"Sorry."

DeNafria turned onto the street leading to the Lincoln Tunnel. "You were in homicide, right?" he asked.

"Eight years," Pavlik said.

"Same partner?"

"Most of the time, yeah."

"He still in homicide?"

"Yep."

"I've been alone until now," DeNafria said. "This is the first time they paired me up. O.C., I mean."

"Will it be a problem?" Pavlik asked.

"Not at all," DeNafria said. "I'm looking forward to the company."

"Right," Pavlik said, still a bit uncomfortable.

They were halfway through the Lincoln Tunnel before either man spoke again.

"We're following up on a loan sharking-slash-extortion situation," DeNafria said. "What we hope will turn into that kind of charge. Some of the names will eventually match the family trees I'm sure you've been looking over. We're out on the extreme edges of those trees. In fact, you're best not even looking at them again for a while. We have a guy, a rich guy wannabe who isn't quite sure what he wants to do with the rest of his life. One Larry Berra, just like Yogi, the Yankee. His father was a big shot associate of the Vignieri's during his day. Import-export, trucking, garbage, the works. He died a year or so ago. Larry's a loner, no brothers or sisters, but he's got a mother with a soft heart, all that leftover mob money, and her son is a loser. Larry never bothered to do the right thing growing up. Somewhere along the line he watched one too many movies and he wanted to be a connected guy. So he bought into the association thing. Except he's not nearly as smart as his father. Every so often he does something really stupid and takes a powder for money he puts out on the streets. Enter Vittorio the barber, from where I just came. A sixty-year-old married zip from the other side, who got himself a Cuban girlfriend thirty years his junior. Lucia Gonzalez is her name. She took Vittorio the barber for a ride with our friend Larry's money. Vittorio reached out to Larry for about sixty grand and came up about sixty grand short."

"Ouch," Pavlik said.

DeNafria smiled. "You still with me?"

"There's more?"

"It never ends," DeNafria said. "So, after Larry makes two or three hundred threatening calls to Vittorio's house and scares the shit out of the old lady, Vittorio's wife, Larry comes to the conclusion he's out the money he sported our friendly barber. And there's really no way in hell he can get it back so we figure he put out a marker for goons. X percent for whatever amount the goons can collect. Which is why I was at Vittorio the barber's house this morning. I don't think they counted on Vittorio calling us but he did. I went to see who the goons were. Two guys I know from the Vignieri crew we watch. Today it was Jimmy Pinto, basically a nobody with some small money on the streets, and Jimmy Bench-Press Mangino, a twice-convicted strong arm guy not afraid of going back. A real animal."

"Nice people," Pavlik said.

"Yes," DeNafria said. "And they'll surprise you at every turn, you give them the chance."

"And we're going to New Jersey for what?" Pavlik asked.

"Oh, Jets tickets," DeNafria said. "I got a thirteen-year-old has never been to a football game. I'm not crazy about going to the Meadowlands to see a New York team, but the Bills are in Buffalo and I don't have the extra time for an eight hour one-way drive."

Pavlik made a face. "You serious, about the Jets tickets?" he asked.

DeNafria shrugged. "Why?"

"I can get you on the forty yard line for face value," Pavlik said. "Maybe for free."

"Yeah?" DeNafria asked. "Great. That would be great. And I'd be more than willing to pay. You don't like football?"

"Hate it," Pavlik said. "It's a faggot sport, all that equipment, the tight pants."

Now DeNafria made the face.

"I used to box," Pavlik said.

"And?"

"It was a joke," Pavlik said. "I'm just not into football."

"Hey," DeNafria said. "Whatever turns you on."

When they were out of the Lincoln Tunnel, DeNafria turned left and drove between evenly spaced rows of orange rubber traffic cones for the eastbound tube of the tunnel.

"I'll go see Ms. Lucia Gonzalez," DeNafria said.

"Just like the Cuban kid," Pavlik said. "Elian."

DeNafria looked confused. "Huh? Oh, right," he said. "The kid in Miami."

"I really was joking about the football thing," Pavlik said.

"Huh? Oh, yeah. No problem."

Both men were uncomfortable. Pavlik said, "So you're going to see Lucia."

"Right," DeNafria said. "Vittorio was pretty anxious to give her up once the threats started. I'm guessing they didn't part as friends."

"And what should I do?" Pavlik asked. "You want me to continue to familiarize myself with these guys or what?"

"Who's on the list they gave you?" DeNafria asked.

Pavlik squinted as he thought about it. "Pete the plumber," he said. "Or was it Pizza Pete?"

DeNafria smiled. "Both," he said.

"And Tony Pug," Pavlik said. "That sound right?"

"Yep," DeNafria said. He switched lanes inside the tunnel when the van in front of him slowed down. "He has this dog, a pug, he walks everywhere with. He's not a made guy, none of those guys you mentioned are, but they're longtime associates. Some of the money guys behind the wiseguys. Tony Pug is deep in porn. He took over where Charlie Rega left off. You heard of Rega, right?"

"The wiseguy killed on the Canarsie pier," Pavlik said.

"The same," DeNafria said. "A nasty piece of work."

"You sure you don't need me with the woman?" Pavlik asked.

"You're more valuable as a beard with her. You can get a lot closer she doesn't know your face."

"The story of my life," Pavlik said.

DeNafria laughed. "Now that's funny," he said.

Pavlik rolled his eyes.

Chapter 3

"How's Gene?" Benjamin Luchessi asked.

"He's a jerkoff," Mangino said.

Luchessi was a thin man with a thick head of gray hair he combed straight back. He wore black slacks, a white polo shirt and blue tinted sunglasses. They were in his daughter's Ford Mustang. It was still dripping soap and water from the car wash Luchessi had just drove it through. They were heading west on the Belt Parkway. The back windows were opened. The sound of the wind was fairly loud inside the car.

"He's a genuine bed wetter, Gene is," Luchessi said. "He didn't go back on the junk, he had himself a nice home there in the hotel."

"He mentioned the end of the week," Mangino said. "Friday or Saturday, if that helps."

"It does," Luchessi said. "It's sooner than I anticipated but it works just as good. The poor fuck, he'll never know what hit him."

Mangino fumbled a cigarette from a pack. Luchessi grabbed his lighter from the console and lit the cigarette for Mangino.

"Thanks," Mangino said.

"Gene tell you I'm the one recommended you?" Luchessi asked.

"He was too busy bragging about his newfound wealth."

"Yeah, well, I hope he enjoyed it."

Mangino opened his window a crack. He took a drag on the cigarette and exhaled toward the opening. He said, "This other thing you need me for today, I was hoping it earns me a final stripe. No disrespect intended, but I think I'm overdue here. Between whatever it is you need me for and the last stretch I did."

Luchessi patted Mangino's leg. "It's a formality, kid," he said. "I need a skipper's approval, but this thing you're doing tonight is for a skipper. It's academic after this."

"I was starting to wonder was my day ever coming," Mangino said. "I mean, some guys I know, well, they just aren't genuine. At least they didn't earn it genuine. Again, no disrespect intended, but there's guys out there with buttons couldn't make first team crossing guards."

"Tell me about it," Luchessi said. "It's a sign of the times, what's going on today. A lot of shit slips through the cracks. And a lot of guys, good earners especially, they don't want anything to do with it anymore. You read the papers, you can't blame them. I'm not so sure I'd want in myself. Not if I was just starting out and I knew better."

"Except there's nothing else for me," Mangino said. "One too many priors. Two stretches now. And I can't cut hair."

Luchessi laughed. "I know a guy, good earner, got sent away for fifteen months, gave it all up, his street money, when he come out, to cut hair. And he was a damn good earner. He ain't rich now, he's making a living, but he's not sweating who's making a deal to give him up either. The price of peace of mind, I guess, cutting hair."

"It's still not for me," Mangino said.

"And then there's the Larry Berra's of the world," Luchessi continued. "Speaking of which, you'll have a meeting with him tomorrow night. If you're lucky, the piece of tail he sports will be there, too. She's a looker."

Mangino picked his teeth with the cover from a book of matches. "He as stupid as I hear?" he asked.

Luchessi chuckled. "I used to do business with his old man. The guy was sharp. I knew enough not to bleed him too bad. He was an earner. He had long arms. Friends everywhere. The kid is a birth defect when it comes to money. Especially making it. I mean, who the fuck gives fifty-eight large to a barber? Answer? Larry does. He's getting too stupid to leave alone. I don't look after it for him, the money he tosses around out there, some other fucking barber will. You see what I'm saying?"

"I hear you," Mangino said.

"So don't spook him tomorrow night," Luchessi said. "Give him a stroke job. The key to a kid like Larry is helping him believe the lie he's living. You'll have to bite your tongue every now and then but it'll be worth your effort, you play him right. Let's face it, his time has come. We don't bleed this kid now, sooner or later somebody else will."

Luchessi turned off the Belt Parkway at Bay Parkway. He parked along the service road and lit a fresh cigarette. He took a couple of drags, closed his window and turned up the radio. He leaned in toward Mangino and spoke just above a whisper. "In the movie they say, 'I got a stone in my shoe.'"

"Which movie is that?" Mangino asked.

"*The Godfather,* the last one. The one with the good-looking kid, Andy Garcia."

"I didn't see that one."

"This friend of mine," Luchessi continued. "The one's gonna

speak up for you when the time comes, he needs this stone removed from his shoe."

Mangino didn't flinch.

Luchessi opened the glove compartment. He pointed to a key ring with two keys on it. "There's a blue minivan at the end of the block up ahead. Under the seat is a piece with a muffler. A twenty-five. I suggest you lose them both soon as you're finished."

Mangino took the keys from the glove compartment. "What time is good?" he asked.

"After dark," Luchessi said. "The minivan won't be reported until tomorrow morning so you have all night."

Mangino remained still and waited for further instructions.

"You take the Belt Parkway back east to Canarsie," Luchessi continued. "Here's the address." He handed Mangino a scribbled address on a yellow piece of paper.

"I think I know the area," Mangino said.

"He's in an illegal apartment in the garage," Luchessi said. "The door is behind the stoop, directly across from where they put the garbage cans." He handed Mangino a picture of a well-dressed young man with blond hair. "He's a flaky fag so he may or may not come to his door. And there may or may not be someone with him. I doubt it, since he's in hiding, but you never know with these people. Very fucking promiscuous. They gotta get out and have a smoke on the baloney pony every so often, remind themselves they're fags."

Mangino lit a cigarette. "His name is Brian," Luchessi continued. "He's got short blond hair, blue eyes, and a huge dick, although I doubt he comes to the door naked."

Mangino smiled.

Luchessi waved a finger. "It's no joke," he said. "You wanna be sure you got the right one, check his pants after you whack him. Kid's got a cock gotta be twelve-fourteen inches."

Mangino was impressed. "God bless," he said.

Luchessi waved it off. "Every inch a waste," he said. "Unless you're him. He's ambidextrous or some shit. Could give himself blow jobs."

"I won't ask how you know this," Mangino said.

"He was the guy running the show at the Brooklyn Inn before our bald-headed, big-eared friend, Eugene," Luchessi said. "Except he starred in half the movies he made and he used kids in half the others. You got no idea what that kiddy porn shit has brought down on us. It's a fucking cancer the public wants removed. Personally, I agree. Leave it for the Chinks and Spanish gangs. We stay out of that shit, we do ourselves a big favor. Except some guys didn't like letting go of a good thing. Our own guys, I'm talking about. There was a lotta money in that sick shit. Those guys are dead now, most of them. You read about the bodies off the Canarsie pier a few weeks back? That was them. Jerry Capeci's article called it spring-cleaning for the mob or some shit and he wasn't so far from the truth. The fag, Brian, was involved with some psycho pedophile-killer, Timothy Waller. Him I know you heard about. He was in all the papers since they pinched him. Kidnapped, raped, and killed kids for fun. Killed more than a dozen. Raped hundreds, what he admitted to. The psycho even filmed some of it. Imagine, torturing kids on film? Cocksucker finally picked on a kid somebody gave a fuck about, some rich couple on Long Island. They got the feds involved. Some local cop made the bust and saved the kid. Only, none of our people had a clue about anything between Brian the fag and this Waller psycho. They were onetime lovers or some shit. So now Brian claims he has something this Waller psycho did on film at the Brooklyn Inn. He had the balls to threaten our friend with this information. We found him because some broad in the D.A.'s office, some word processor or some shit, is banging somebody on one of our crews. Our fag friend, Brian, he's on some potential witness list in an O.C. file."

"The stone in some skipper's shoe," Mangino said.

"Needs to be removed," Luchessi said.

Mangino shrugged. "So, I'll shoot him in the fucking head," he said.

Later the same night, Mangino parked the minivan in front of a Catholic school two blocks from the address on Canarsie Road. He wore thin black cycling gloves, black slacks, a navy-blue turtleneck, a black windbreaker, and dark sunglasses. A shoulder length black wig covered his head.

He had taped the .25mm Raven and the silencer with black electric tape. Assembled, the weapon fit comfortably inside the waist of his slacks under the windbreaker.

He crossed the street to avoid direct contact with a dog walker. He glanced up at the windows of the home, then turned into the driveway and headed for the door to the illegal apartment. He looked around once before ringing the bell. He could hear music from inside the apartment.

He rang the bell again and the front door suddenly opened. A handsome young man with blond hair stood there. He wore a blue polo shirt and white shorts. He smiled coyly at Mangino, as he looked him over.

"Hi," the blond-haired man said.

Mangino smiled back. "You Brian?" he asked.

The blond-haired man licked his lips and looked Mangino up and down. "That depends," he said. "Who're you, big boy?"

"I'm a big boy," Mangino said, then he pushed the blond man hard into the apartment. He carefully closed and locked the door behind him and pulled the .25mm from inside the waist of his pants. The blond man was on the floor trying to scramble to his feet when Mangino extended his arm and fired four shots. The blond-haired man was dead before Mangino fired two more into his forehead.

Mangino went down on one knee and reached for the dead man's pants. He pulled the front open and tugged down on the white shorts. When Mangino saw the large penis, he squinted as he whispered: "Jesus fucking Christ."

Chapter 4

Robert Downs, the police commissioner of New York City, held a remote in his right hand and stared intently at the television screen. Michael McDonald, a union officer and representative of the Patrolmen's Benevolent Association, sat with a notepad on his lap and also watched the television. Both men were in an empty conference room at One Police Plaza. McDonald fidgeted with a pen as he glanced down at his notes.

The screen flashed and the video showed two men at a distance. A tall man with broad shoulders threw measured uppercut punches into the belly of a bloody man. The bloody man was pinned in the corner between two walls. He sagged with each new punch until he nearly toppled over. The tall man picked the bloody man back up and resumed the attack.

"Why is it Detective Pavlik isn't in jail right now?" Commissioner Downs asked.

"Luck," McDonald said. "And discretion. Remember whom Pavlik is punching there. Timothy Waller. Remember what Timothy Waller did. And the fact Timothy Waller is still alive. He didn't die from that beating."

Downs stopped the video with the remote. He turned to

McDonald. "Do you really think I could go to the press with that explanation?" he asked.

"Which is why the press doesn't know a thing about this tape," McDonald said. "Because we have the cooperation of the FBI and the Vignieri crime family with this."

Downs waved the last remark off. "The FBI and the Vignieri's? Please."

"Think about this for a minute," McDonald said. "Timothy Waller is behind bars on federal charges we deferred to because it was their case. But everybody involved, including what the press has been spoon-fed, knows this was a New York City homicide cop putting in extra hours, doing his job above and beyond the call of duty, who made the bust. This was the stuff of gold shields, Commissioner. We took a lot of well deserved glory for this, all of us, and we'll compromise the official case behind closed doors because of Detective Pavlik's actions, but the bottom line is the world knows Detective Pavlik as a hero right now. I don't know that we want to change that image. What we have in mind instead is a tit-for-tat exchange to defer. This was about snuff films and child pornography. Those are very hot issues thanks to the Internet, CNN, and the local media. Even the mob can't afford direct links to that stuff anymore. Behind the doors, yes, some mobsters might traffic in that venue but the mainstay goombahs trying to hold on can't afford this kind of publicity, not child pornography or snuff. The mob put the lid on this pronto, soon as the feds moved in. Three of their main traffickers were found floating off the Canarsie pier the next morning. They washed their hands of it before anybody else could do it for them."

Downs was cleaning a fingernail with a pen cap. "And what about the next goombah decides to go public with a federal deal to build pools in the desert someplace?" he asked. "What about that?"

McDonald shrugged. "Sour grapes," he said. "There are only a few wiseguys involved in this thing anyway. They can bring it up, that they know of, or heard of, a New York homicide detective lost it on Timothy Waller but who's gonna care? Timothy Waller isn't even bringing it up. Fact is, if the mob can reach Waller inside the joint, he's a dead man anyway."

Downs huffed as he reached for a cup of coffee.

"If we nail Pavlik for something like this, we lose a damn good detective," McDonald said. "We also besmirch all the glory he just took credit for. Glory we all can use right now. And for what?" He pointed at the blank television screen. "Lets face it," he continued, "for five or ten minutes there, Timothy Waller got something of what he deserves for fucking and killing kids on camera so he could sell sick films to rich psychos with nothing better to do with their money. For five or ten minutes there, Timothy Waller was getting some justice."

"And how do we know Detective Pavlik doesn't lose it again someday and come back to haunt us the same way?" Downs asked. "I came up through the ranks so I know the inside story on this kind of thing. I can recognize a good cop when I see one but I can also recognize compulsive obsessive behavior. I don't doubt the detective's moral convictions or his desire to see justice done, but the bottom line is, it's not his job to take it to the next level."

"Granted," McDonald said. "We put him in O.C."

Downs turned on his desk lamp. He squinted from the glare. "Organized crime," he said as he started to nod.

"It's the perfect place for Pavlik," McDonald continued. "He's been studying crime family charts the last few days. Familiarizing himself with the various crews he'll be investigating. What the hell kind of trouble can he get himself in there? All they do is sit around and watch wiseguys eat and drink."

Downs turned the lamp off. "That's all they do, huh?"

"Pretty much, yeah. We put him with a guy working solo until now. John DeNafria."

Downs looked shocked. "Eastern Parkway, John DeNafria? The guy shot the kid at the ATM?"

"It was self-defense," McDonald said. "Verified by a camera."

"That guy brought the entire black community knocking on city hall's doors," Downs said. "My God, man, don't you remember?" He was scratching the back of his head. "Well I do, if you don't," he continued. "'Jesus Christ was a proud black man and your white detective just shot and killed one of his blessed children.' That is more or less a direct quote of the esteemed reverend."

"Detective DeNafria was also cleared of any wrongdoing," McDonald said.

Downs leaned forward in his chair. "Holy shit, McDonald," he said. "You PBA people have bigger balls than I do. Much bigger balls."

"DeNafria was shot at several times before returning fire," McDonald said. "Lucky for him, and us, it was all caught on that ATM camera. It was self-defense. There was never any question about that."

"Except they put the poor bastard on trial, didn't they?"

McDonald half shrugged. "The mayor is your boss, Bob."

"That's right," Downs said. "It's a fickle fucking world, politics. Don't forget it."

"DeNafria has lived a very quiet existence in O.C. ever since," McDonald continued. "He's the perfect match for our hero detective. He's been briefed. He knows how to handle Pavlik."

Downs seemed to be thinking about it. He took a few deep breaths, pointed a finger at McDonald and said: "Fine. Fine. You got it. We'll do it your way, the PBA way. Since Detectives DeNafria and Pavlik will make such good partners, put it in writing, your recommendation for Detective Pavlik's promotion to gold shield. Since what he did is the stuff of gold shields, let's give him one. In fact, I want your boss's signature on that recommendation as well. The same goes for his recommendation for a transfer. I want both names on it, you and your boss. Since the PBA couldn't resist the police commissioner seeing a VCR tape the FBI rammed down your throats, and I just saw it, most of it, you guys can handle this one. I'll be there at the ceremony standing side-by-side with the mayor, and we'll both give Detective Pavlik the public blowjob he deserves for catching Timothy Waller, but the PBA, in all its glory, will be there, too. From this moment forward, he's a hero about to transfer from one department to another. God bless him and God bless New York and God bless America. One more notch in the mayor's belt for his trip to Albany someday. Crime is down and the Timothy Wallers of the world do deserve a few rounds with a former prizefighter. But now the pendulum swings back the other way, my friend. You owe us one. Remember that."

McDonald swallowed hard. "Sure, Bob," he said. "Of course."

Downs was up out of his chair. He started to turn away when he remembered the VCR tape. "And take that tape with you when you leave," he said. "I never want to hear about it again, much less see it."

"Right," McDonald said.

"Burn it, you got any brains, you and your boss."

"Right," McDonald said. "Of course."

Chapter 5

Aelish Phalen held the pug in her lap and scratched at its barrel chest with her free hand. She was an attractive woman at thirty-nine years of age. Her skin was fair and spotted with freckles. She had bright green eyes and thick full lips. She had just stretched after a long jog. Her long blond hair was still wet with sweat. She stopped a moment and draped a towel around her neck.

Detective Alex Pavlik rubbed at the knuckles on his right hand. He could see a bruise forming on two of them. He opened and closed his right hand several times while he watched his girlfriend play with the dog he had brought home a few minutes earlier.

Aelish looked up at her boyfriend from the floor. "She's adorable, love," she said with a hint of her native Irish accent.

"She's stolen property," he said.

"She's what?" Aelish asked. She stopped scratching the dog.

"It's a long story," Pavlik said.

"Well, tell me," Aelish said as she struggled to stand up without putting the dog down. "I'm not going anywhere."

Pavlik stopped rubbing his knuckles. "Some guy was kicking it," he said. "The guy I was watching. Some ginzo wannabe around the crew I'm supposed to be familiarizing myself with. He had this dog with him and he kept kicking it. The dog was terrified was why it didn't move. The fat prick kept pulling and tugging on the leash. Hard, too. The dog was scared. It cowered. Then the tough guy started to kick it. I couldn't stand to watch anymore."

Aelish pointed at his hand. "And that's why you were rubbing your hand, is it? Because you didn't just take the dog. You hit the man, didn't you?"

Pavlik shrugged. "The fat slob I was watching, yeah. What's it weigh, all of ten pounds?"

Aelish held the dog up close to her face and kissed it. "She can use a bath," she said.

Pavlik rubbed at his bruised knuckles again. "I didn't go to town on him or anything," he said. "I just walked up to him and nailed him one in the stomach. Knocked his wind out. He lost his breath and went right down to his knees."

"That wouldn't hurt your hand," Aelish said. "Punching a fat man in the lard."

Pavlik tried to crack his knuckles and flinched from the pain. "Shit" he said.

Aelish was waiting for an answer. "Well?"

"I picked up the dog and saw it was terrified," he said. "Then I turned and cracked the slob one in the jaw. It was like granite."

Aelish giggled as she scratched the dog's chest. "Serves you right," she said. She set the dog on the floor.

"I don't think anyone saw me," Pavlik continued. "Especially since I was the surveillance. My partner went off to do something else. I was alone. I don't think there was anybody else watching. Unless it was the feds."

"That's a scary thought," Aelish said. "The FBI."

Pavlik tried to change the subject. "I mention my partner is a guinea?" he asked. "First it was Green, a black guy, and now it's an Italian."

"This isn't a funny situation," Aelish said. "Maybe you should call Dexter and ask him what to do."

Pavlik waved a finger. "Uh-uh," he said. "I'd cut my balls off before I give Dex that kind of satisfaction."

Aelish set her hands on her hips.

"Anyway, DeNafria, my new partner, he's alright, I think," Pavlik said. "He went through a mess of his own a few years back. Killed a black kid in a shootout. He was up on charges and had the entire black community breathing down his neck. I'm wondering they don't put all the fuckups, the headaches like myself, in O.C. just to keep us quiet."

"Or to save your jobs," Aelish said.

"Please," Pavlik said. "I don't think they're that considerate."

The dog started to cry. It was looking up at Aelish from the floor. She bent at the waist to pick the dog up again. She cradled it against her chest and kissed its head.

Pavlik pointed at his girlfriend. "When you bend over like that, you got a nice ass," he said.

"Only when I bend?"

"No, all the time. It's just a lot easier to notice when you bend over."

"Did anyone see you take the dog?" Aelish asked.

Pavlik was confused a moment. "Huh? Oh, no. I don't think so."

"You hope not," Aelish said.

"Nobody saw anything," Pavlik said. "I jumped in a taxi and got out of there."

Aelish turned the dog over in her arms and scratched at the

beige belly. "And now the dog is ours?" she asked without looking at her boyfriend.

"It was your birthday last week," Pavlik said.

"You gave me a beautiful pair of earrings," Aelish said.

"And some lingerie."

"Yes, those as well."

"So now you have a dog."

"Except it isn't yours to give."

"I'm not bringing it back," Pavlik said. "Even if I could, I mean. I can't, but even if I could I wouldn't. No way."

"Are you sure this won't become an issue with the police force?" Aelish asked. "Maybe you should turn it in to an animal shelter or something. Just in case somebody did see you."

"No way," Pavlik said. "They'll just kill it if nobody adopts it. No, we'll keep it."

"And who will walk it, love?" Aelish asked.

"Both of us," Pavlik said.

"You sure?"

"Sure I'm sure."

Aelish kissed the dog and set it down again. It immediately started to cry. Aelish waved a finger at Pavlik.

"I think she wants you," he said.

"I think I've caught some of the blarney," Aelish said. She scooped the dog up one more time.

"You still have a nice ass," Pavlik said.

"What about a name? What will we call her?"

"Lucky," Pavlik suggested. "That's what she is."

"She's also stolen property," Aelish said. "I don't suppose we can call her that now."

Pavlik closed his eyes in imitation of thought. When he opened them, Aelish had shifted her weight onto one leg. She was staring at him.

"What?" he said.

"Well?"

"Natasha," he said.

"And where'd you get that one?"

"I used to like the cartoon when I was a kid," he said. "Boris Badenough and Natasha. The Bulwinkle cartoon. Rocky and Bulwinkle."

"Sorry, love, I'm not familiar with it."

Pavlik pointed at Aelish again. "Don't worry," he said. "Natasha had a nice ass, too."

Chapter 6

Lucia Gonzalez was short and busty. She had thick muscular thighs and a full figure. Her short curly hair was dyed golden blond. She wore tight-fitted black slacks, a white ruffled blouse, and three-inch spiked high heels. She sat at the small bar inside TAPAZ, TAPAZ, TAPAZ, the Spanish restaurant she owned, reading the *Daily News* while the bartender moved boxes of produce from the delivery drop, just inside the restaurant, down to the basement.

Detective DeNafria was directed to the woman at the bar by the bartender. The restaurant was preparing for the day's business. It was just after ten o'clock in the morning. DeNafria showed his badge to the woman and sat on the stool at the corner of the small bar so he could see her face without having to turn his head to one side. The woman closed the newspaper as DeNafria opened his notepad on the bar.

"I'm Lucia Gonzalez," she said. "What's this about, please?" She spoke with a slight Hispanic accent. She had a husky voice for a small woman.

"You have a friend named Vittorio," DeNafria said. "He's a barber."

Lucia held up a finger. "Had a friend," she said. "We no longer speak."

DeNafria ignored her. "He borrowed money for you to open a restaurant. This the place?"

Lucia spoke without looking at DeNafria. "He helped me with some back rent," she said. "I'm going to pay him back."

"But you were involved, right?"

Now Lucia held up two fingers. "Twice," she said. "Two time. He want more from the relationship but it was a mistake. My mistake."

"Funny," DeNafria said. "Vittorio says the same thing about it being a mistake."

Lucia finally looked up at DeNafria. The telephone rang. Lucia glanced back at the phone at the end of the bar, and then yelled at the bartender to answer it.

"Sorry," she said to DeNafria. "That's all that happened, Detective. Vittorio was a cute old man. I was rebounding from my boyfriend. Like I said, it was a mistake."

"Is Grampa!" the bartender yelled from the basement.

Lucia looked confused. "Excuse me," she told DeNafria. She turned on the stool and yelled back: "Who?"

"Your new boyfriend!" the bartender yelled back.

Lucia blushed. DeNafria raised his eyebrows at her.

"Tell him I call him back!" she yelled.

Lucia fumbled a cigarette from a pack on the bar. DeNafria offered her a light. Lucia acknowledged the light with a nod of the head.

"You running a game, Lucy?" DeNafria asked.

"Lucia," she said. "What do you mean?"

"You and old men and this restaurant," DeNafria explained. "You taking old fools for a ride?"

Lucia slapped the bar top. "That is a terrible accusation,

Detective," she said. "No. The answer is no, I no running a game."

"Did you know where Vittorio got the money? The fifty-eight thousand he borrowed?"

"No."

"Why don't I believe you?"

"Believe what you want."

DeNafria moved her ashtray to get Lucia's attention. "A wannabe mobster, which in some cases is worse than the real thing," he told her. "Larry Berra. I'm sure you met him. I'm sure he came here for public stroke jobs."

"Don't talk to me like that, please," Lucia said.

"Right," DeNafria said. "Anyway, Larry is the kind of wannabe that can't do the things he wishes he could do, like be a tough guy, for instance. He's too soft. He comes from money. He has to pretend. And he probably watches too much television to know how it really works. Maybe that HBO thing is his favorite show, I don't know. Do you watch it, the HBO show?"

"I don't know what you're talking about," she said.

"Right," DeNafria continued. "Of course you don't. The point being, Larry is the type who sends people, goons, to do his dirty work. Which is what he's done to Vittorio now. Larry has sent a couple of goons to the old man's house."

Lucia was nervous. She said, "Vittorio told me he re-mortgaged his house. I don't know about any Larry."

"That was his money, the money he got from his re-mortgage. But the rest of it, the last fifty-eight thousand, that came from Larry, probably at three points a week, which is a fortune to try and pay off. So Vittorio couldn't pay it off and now Larry wants his money back. He's sending goons to Vittorio's house."

"Did something happen to Vito?" Lucia asked, suddenly concerned.

"Would you really give a shit?" DeNafria asked.

Lucia turned away from him. "I liked Vito," she said. "He was a nice old man."

"Nice enough to mortgage his house for you, I know," DeNafria said.

Lucia wheeled on DeNafria. "I didn't make him do that," she said. "He offer to help me. He was nice man. He brought me the money."

"And you know where he got the other money," DeNafria said. "You know everything I'm talking about, lady."

Lucia looked away from him again.

DeNafria leaned in closer to her. "Yeah, well, should anything happen to Vittorio, excuse me, Vito, somebody will come to see you," he said. "Either us, the law. Or them, the goons. Larry is going to still want his money and we're going to want to prosecute whoever does anything to Vittorio. Can you understand that?"

"What are you saying, please?" Lucia said. "I told you I don't know anything. And I am very busy in the restaurant. I have to open in an hour."

DeNafria looked around the place. "Yeah," he said, "I can see."

"What do you want?"

"I want you to record the man who's sending the goons to Vittorio's house. I want the man who gave Vitto the money, Larry Berra. I need you to file a report with us if he threatens you."

Lucia made a face. "You want me to antagonize a Mafioso?" she asked. "Are you crazy? I didn't borrow that money."

"Vittorio did, I know," DeNafria said. "He borrowed it for you."

"I'm not getting involved, Detective, no way," Lucia said, waving her right hand over her shoulder. "Not with Mafioso."

"Then I'll need the name of your new boyfriend, please," DeNafria said. "You remember, grandpa, I think your guy called him."

Lucia turned and glared at him.

DeNafria turned on the stool and glared back. "Look, Ms. Gonzalez, I can go back the last few years on you and this place and however many other old men you befriended, took their money and then dumped. They aren't easy to prosecute but there are laws regarding that sort of thing. It becomes a little easier when there's a pattern established."

Lucia didn't flinch. She spoke through half-clenched teeth. "What do I have to do?"

"Get him to talk," DeNafria said. He pointed to the telephone at the end of the bar. "On that."

Lucia glanced back at the phone.

"Tonight," DeNafria added. He waited until she was looking at him again. "Tonight," he repeated.

Chapter 7

Larry Berra sat with his girlfriend at a secluded table in the garden at Borolla restaurant on West Street in Greenwich Village. Berra was a thirty-year-old chubby man. He had dark hair and thin lips. His complexion was dark from tanning. He wore black slacks, a gray polo shirt, and a black blazer. He also wore gold, a lot of it. His Rolex was the forty-thousand-dollar Presidential model. The eighteen-karat solid gold bracelet and matching neck chain were worth another five thousand. The ring on his right hand was a two-karat diamond in a platinum setting.

Berra's girlfriend, Leanna Flynn, was twenty-six years old, tall and thin and beautiful. She had long brown hair that reached the top of her hips when she stood up. Her breasts were mostly implants but the symmetry was a perfect match with her twenty-two-inch waist and her thirty-four-inch hips. Tonight she was dressed in a red leather miniskirt with matching high heels. She wore a tight navy-blue top that hugged her breasts. Her hair was tied behind her in a long ponytail.

It was half-past eight o'clock and they were arguing. They were drinking red wine. Berra lit his Macanudo Churchill cigar while Leanna flirted with one of the waiters she recognized from her gym.

Berra glanced at his watch before sipping his wine. "Where the fuck is this guy?" he said.

"If he's a convict, maybe he got arrested on his way over," Leanna said, rubbing it in.

"That's not funny," Berra said. "I'm gonna put him on that thing out in Brooklyn. That motherfucker that owes me sixty grand."

Leanna rolled her eyes. "You're going to pay him, Larry," she said. "Stop talking like a gangster. There's nobody here to impress."

"Hey, you got a big fuckin mouth, you know that?" Berra said. He was glaring at his girlfriend.

A large shadow crossed the table. "Jesus Christ," Leanna said. Her eyes opened wide. She was looking up at a man with broad shoulders and thick arms. He was wearing a tight black sweater and black slacks.

"Mr. Berra?" the big man said.

Berra's eyes opened as wide as his girlfriend's. He stood up slowly from his chair. "Jimmy Bench-Press?" he asked.

The big man smiled at both Berra and Leanna. "Is it alright if I sit?" he asked.

Berra extended his hand across the table. "Yeah, sure, of course," he said. "This is my girlfriend, Leanna Flynn. Leanna, Jimmy Bench-Press."

"Mangino," the big man said. "Jimmy Mangino."

Leanna leaned into her boyfriend. "Now I'm impressed," she said.

Both men sat down. Leanna smiled at Mangino. Berra saw the smile and nudged her with his knee under the table.

"What?" Leanna asked Berra, annoyed.

Berra glared at her again. Leanna stood up. "I'm going to let you two talk while I clean up," she said. "I need cigarettes anyway."

Berra pulled a ten-dollar bill from a wad of cash in his right pants pocket. "Get me a Marlboro," he told Leanna. "Jimmy? You need anything?"

"No thanks," Mangino said to Leanna. "Thanks anyway."

Both men watched Leanna Flynn walk away. Berra said, "Some piece of ass, huh?"

Mangino was surprised. "She's a very pretty girl," he said.

Berra rolled his eyes as he poured a glass of wine for Mangino. "She's just another cunt," he said, waving her off. "Jimmy Pinto said you just got out."

Mangino held his glass up to Berra. Both men clinked glasses and said: "Salute."

"Month ago," Mangino said.

"So you need work, right?"

Mangino shrugged. "I'm looking into things," he said.

"But no luck on that other thing out in Brooklyn," Berra said.

"I was a little hampered," Mangino said.

Berra was about to sip his wine. He stopped to listen. "How so?"

Mangino leaned forward in his chair. "It's nothing personal," he said.

"Jimmy Pinto?" Berra asked.

"He's a nice enough guy and all," Mangino said. "Don't get me wrong. But these two people we can go after for your money, from what I was told about it, they're not the type Jimmy can handle, if you know what I mean. Jimmy isn't used to that sort of thing, the rough stuff. A woman and an old man, I mean."

Berra leaned in closer to Mangino. "What would you have done different?" he asked.

"Something," Mangino said as he sat back. "I wouldn't have talked to the wife, for one thing. I mean, fifty-eight K is a lot of money. Unless the old lady borrowed it, what's the point talking to her?"

"So, what would you have done?" Berra asked again.

"Pushed my way in," Mangino said. "We didn't even try the door to see if it was locked. Toss something through the window. There was patio furniture or something there. A garbage can. Like I said, I would've did something. Before I broke one of the old man's legs."

Berra swallowed hard and forced a smile. Both men sipped their wine.

Mangino looked Berra in the eyes. "I can handle it if you want," he said.

"You're telling me you can hurt the old man," Berra said. "How can you get my money?"

"That's my business," Mangino said. "Post me half the money up front, to get me started, and I can make you a guarantee on the balance."

Berra forced himself to laugh. "Half?" he said through the phony laugh. "Tell me I don't look that stupid. Please."

"Thirty percent then," Mangino said. He sipped his wine again.

"And what's your guarantee," Berra asked.

"A body part," Mangino said as he leaned forward again. "Something you can see. But for fifty percent, I give you the whole enchilada. I'll whack one of them. Your choice which."

Berra's eyes opened wide again. "That might be going a little far," he said.

"That's the difference in economics," Mangino said. "Where you're sitting and where I'm sitting. I'd have no problem taking care of things for that kind of scratch, fifty-eight large. Right now, for fifty-eight thousand, I'd go after their ancestors."

Berra swallowed hard again. He reached for his glass of water. "I might be interested in the thirty percent proposition," he said. "As a matter of respect, of course. Which one would you go after for the money? If you have to choose."

"If the barber used the money for his girlfriend, then she's the one with the money," Mangino said. "Even if she spent it, if she stung him, she can sting somebody else."

Berra glanced around the restaurant. "How do you feel about dealing with a woman?" he asked in a whisper.

Mangino picked at a cuticle on one of his pinky fingers. "You know that old saying, old enough to bleed, old enough to butcher?" Berra nodded. Mangino held his glass up again. "That's how I feel," he said.

Berra completed the toast with his glass. "I'll let you know," he said.

"That's all a man can ask," Mangino said.

Chapter 8

"How's the new guy?" Detective Dexter Greene asked his former partner, Alex Pavlik.

They were standing on the stoop to Greene's front porch in Canarsie. It was a small two-family house with a long driveway and a two-car garage. Greene had bought the house two years earlier. Pavlik had helped Greene paint the outside of the house the following summer. A tiny patch of grass alongside the driveway buffered the front of the house. One of Greene's three sons was playing with a Nerf football in the front yard. The six-year-old kicked the ball around the small yard over and over.

Pavlik pointed to Greene's son. "He likes football," he said. "My new partner, I mean."

"Don't make him a bad person," Greene said. "My new guy is a girl. Arlene Belzinger, if you can believe it. From vice. A looker but . . . well, you know."

"She's white," Pavlik said.

"Yeah," Greene said. "Yours, too?"

"And he's got a kid," Pavlik said. "Likes Jets games. I was coming over for a pair from your guy with the tickets. Can you get them?"

"I guess so, you already promised them out," Greene said. "Not wasting any time sticking your nose up his ass, huh?"

"We have the same exact amount of time in, give or take a few months," Pavlik said. "Most of mine in homicide and vice. Most of his was in street crimes and O.C."

"He was accused of killing a black kid," Greene said.

"I was told," Pavlik said. "He was also cleared. The kid shot first."

Greene smirked. "That's what they said."

Pavlik held up both his hands. "Hey, I'm lucky they didn't can my ass," he said. "PBA showed me a tape of me beating the shit out of that psycho Waller in the basement I found him. He had a camera rolling. The feds grabbed the tape. I could be doing time right now. I'm biting my tongue. The guy turns out to be a white supremacist, my new partner, trust me, I'll put in for another transfer. But I'm not making waves until I have to."

Greene raised his eyebrows. "I'm just saying," he said. "So you watch yourself."

"He seems alright," Pavlik said.

"You compared dick sizes yet?" Greene asked, and quickly waved it off. "What's the point, you both white."

"Can you get the tickets or not, Holmes?" Pavlik asked.

"I said yeah," Greene said. "Yeah means yeah."

"Thank you."

"You're welcome."

"I gotta go now."

"Don't expect a kiss."

Pavlik forced a smile.

Greene did the same.

Both men flipped each other the finger as soon as Greene's son wasn't looking.

Half-an-hour later, Pavlik met up with DeNafria outside the McDonald's on Cross Bay Boulevard in the Howard Beach section of Queens. DeNafria was waiting at the side entrance to the restaurant. He was wearing a brown sweatshirt and baggy gray sweatpants. Pavlik was still dressed for work. He took off his navy-blue blazer and draped it over the front seat of his car.

"Mangino is inside," DeNafria said. "He's the ape at the table inside the corner window. With two other guys."

Pavlik glanced at the three men. "Who're they?" he asked.

"One's Jimmy Pinto," DeNafria said. "The other one, I think, is a guy named Eugene Tranchatta or Tranchetti or something. Eugene somebody. The bald one with the big ears, looks like Dumbo."

Pavlik looked again until he spotted the bald man. DeNafria tossed the last of his cigarette on the floor.

"What you want to do?" Pavlik asked.

"You think they made us?" DeNafria asked.

Pavlik stepped back and stared at the bald man until he looked up. "They did now," Pavlik said.

"Cops at one o'clock," Eugene Tranchatta said. He took a bite of the fish sandwich he was eating and wiped his mouth with a napkin.

"Who brought them?" Jimmy Pinto asked.

"I've been here almost half-an-hour waiting on you two," Tranchatta said. "Hadda be one of you."

"I was pissing behind a tree before I came in," Jimmy Mangino said. "Maybe they saw me."

"You serious?" Pinto asked.

"No," Mangino said.

"What do you think it's about?" Tranchatta asked Mangino.

Mangino eyeballed Tranchatta. "I don't know," he said.

"Well, maybe we can ask them," Pinto said. "They're coming over here."

DeNafria stood behind Jimmy Mangino. Pavlik stood behind Jimmy Pinto.

"You guys want something?" Tranchatta asked DeNafria.

"I'm a friend of Vittorio Tangorra," Pavlik said. He was staring down at Mangino now. Mangino stared back.

"Yeah, so," Jimmy Pinto said. "Who the fuck is that?"

"Some poor slob being pushed around by a couple of goons," Pavlik continued. "Couple guys fit your description."

"My description?" Tranchatta asked, pointing at himself.

Pavlik shifted his glare from Mangino to Tranchatta. "I don't know who the fuck you are," he said. "Except you got big ears make you look like Dumbo."

Pinto and Mangino laughed.

"Fuck you two," Tranchatta said.

Pavlik pointed at Pinto and Mangino for Tranchatta. "These two bruisers were at the old man's house scaring his sixty-year-old wife," he said. "That's a no-no."

Mangino yawned. Jimmy Pinto leaned his elbows on the small table. "You guys cops?" he asked.

"Why else would they act like tough guys?" Mangino said.

"Excuse me?" Pavlik said.

Mangino puckered his lips at Pavlik.

"You want to take this outside?" Pavlik asked. "I'll leave the badge here, you want."

Mangino removed imaginary crumbs from his chest. "I'd break you in half, pal," he said without looking at Pavlik.

Pavlik started for Mangino but DeNafria stopped him. The two detectives glared at each other. DeNafria guided Pavlik away from the table to the exit. He waited until Pavlik was outside the restaurant before he walked back to the table.

"Tell your friends they're under surveillance," DeNafria said to Tranchatta. "In case they can't figure it out."

"I'll do that," Tranchatta said, jerking his fist up and down.

DeNafria pointed at Tranchatta. "Hey," he said. "That's pretty good. Your mother does it almost exactly that same way. That where you get the ears?"

Pinto and Mangino suppressed another laugh. Tranchatta looked to each of his friends one at a time and frowned.

Out in the parking lot, both detectives walked to where they couldn't be seen. DeNafria spoke first.

"I couldn't let you hit Mangino," he said. "You know that, right?"

Pavlik nodded. "I don't even know if I would have," he said. "But he got to me. I think I was more pissed about that, letting him get to me."

"He's good at it," DeNafria said. "He's also pretty good at thumb bending. The guy bench-presses four hundred pounds."

Pavlik showed teeth.

"I'm not looking to make it a challenge," DeNafria said. "I'm just saying. It's what the guy does for a living. He's an animal, pure and simple. But he's not stupid enough to hit a cop. You have to take that into consideration. Pushing him is one thing. You have to be able to back off when the push doesn't turn to a shove."

Pavlik looked away.

"I'm not trying to lecture you, Alex," DeNafria said.

"Call me Pavlik," Pavlik said.

"Fine. Pavlik it is. I'm not trying to lecture you. I'm just making sure you don't fuck up. Not for something like this, a little roust. We accomplished what we went there to do."

Pavlik finally turned to DeNafria. "And that was?" he asked.

"The woman, Lucia, is the one they'll eventually go after," DeNafria said. "She's the only one can afford to pay the loan off. We just steered them in her direction. Which is good, because we're going to need her cooperation."

Pavlik stood silent.

"You okay?" DeNafria asked.

Pavlik remained silent.

DeNafria held up a hand for attention. "Can you at least say it?"

"I'm okay," Pavlik said, pushing his partner's hand down.

"Thank you," DeNafria said.

"You're welcome," Pavlik said.

Chapter 9

It was just after one o'clock in the morning when Mangino sat at the tiny bar in TAPAZ, TAPAZ, TAPAZ. Mangino was still flying from a line of cocaine he had snorted on his way into the city. He had the sniffles and his eyes were red.

The woman he was there to see was sitting at one end of the tiny bar going through waiter checks. She was dressed in a black and white skirt suit. She wore black thigh-high boots. The bartender, somewhere in his twenties, had opened his shirt at the collar and was stocking fresh glasses in the rack above the bar. He smoked a cigarette. He put the cigarette down to tell Mangino the bar was closed.

"In a little while," Mangino said. "I'm thirsty."

"I'm sorry, sir, but we're closed," the bartender repeated. "I can't serve you."

Mangino got up off the barstool. "Then I'll serve myself," he said.

The woman put up a hand to quiet the bartender as she turned to Mangino. "Sir, please, we've spent most of the day here," she pleaded. "We're closing now."

"Give me a beer," Mangino said. He was glaring at the bartender. The bartender tried his best to look mean. The woman thumbed at Mangino. "Give him a beer," she finally said, then held up a finger. "One," she said. "Just one."

The bartender opened a bottle of Budweiser and set it on a coaster. "Three-fifty," he said.

Mangino stroked the air with a fist and took a long drink from the bottle. He finished half the beer before setting it down again. He belched across the bar and turned on his stool to face the woman.

"You Lucy?" he asked.

"Excuse me?" the woman said.

"Who's asking?" the bartender said.

Mangino glanced up at the bartender and saw he was holding a nightstick. "You going to use that, sonny?" he asked.

"Maybe," the bartender said. He flinched by looking at the woman.

"Look, mister, whoever you are, we don't want any trouble in here," the woman said. "We've just worked a long day. So, please, just leave now. Okay? No charge for the beer."

"He's the one with the club in his hands," Mangino said.

"What do you want, sir?" the woman asked.

"Fifty-eight thousand dollars," Mangino said. "But I don't expect you to have it all now. Just some of it now is enough. A couple grand, say. Or whatever you collected tonight. The cash in the drawer."

The woman glanced up at the bartender. Mangino saw his reflection in a glass on the bar. He moved back off the stool and missed getting cracked with the nightstick by inches. The bartender moved toward the end of the bar but Mangino was already heading there. He slipped a brass knuckle over his right hand and ran behind the right cross he aimed at the bartender's face.

The crack of the bartender's jawbone was loud. The bartender crumpled behind the punch as soon as it landed. Blood oozed from his mouth. The woman was off the stool screaming. She started to run for the door when Mangino grabbed her hair. He ran her face first into the edge of a table. He could hear her teeth crack from the contact. He let her go and she sat down hard between two chairs. Her eyes were glazed from shock. She spit fragments of her front teeth onto her lap. Blood flowed from her mouth onto her blouse.

Mangino emptied the register of whatever cash was there, rifled through the bartender's pants pockets and the woman's purse. He left TAPAZ, TAPAZ, TAPAZ, just ten minutes after he first sat at the bar. At the door, he looked over his shoulder and smiled at the woman. "No charge for the facial," he said.

"That was a pretty slick move, handing me your beeper number on a napkin," Leanna Flynn said.

She had come to the door in a blue and white football jersey and navy blue bikini panties. She let Jimmy Mangino inside her apartment and poured herself a cup of coffee.

It was a small one-bedroom apartment in the Murray Hill section of Manhattan. The living room was furnished with a white leather couch, a matching armchair, a glass coffee table, and a black throw rug. A nineteen-inch television sat in the middle of a small black wall unit. The bedroom was off to the right of the living room. The tiny kitchen was off to the left of the apartment door.

Mangino stood in the middle of the living room looking the place over. "Larry pay for this?" he asked.

"Some of it," Leanna said. "We're not that close and I have a job."

"Let me guess," Mangino said. "You're a dancer."

"I'm a hostess," Leanna said. "At a friend of Larry's restaurant close to here on the East Side. I don't strain myself. I work two nights a week."

Mangino let himself drop onto the couch. "Nice and soft," he said.

"Make yourself comfortable," Leanna said. She shifted her weight onto one foot.

Mangino patted a spot next to him on the couch.

"That was very risky," she said. "The beeper thing. What if I told him?"

"I had a hunch about you," Mangino said.

"Really?" Leanna said.

"You like big guys," he said. "Larry's a fat boy but he's big. I saw the way you looked at me. You like big. Am I right or am I right?"

Leanna sipped her coffee. "You're very sure of yourself," she said.

Mangino patted the couch again. "Yes," he said. "Now, you want to be taken or you the type likes to ride on top?"

They had mostly rough sex for the next hour. Both of them reached orgasm more than once. Both of them were exhausted when they were finished. When the telephone rang just before midnight, Leanna answered it while Mangino poured himself a cup of coffee in the kitchen. When Mangino returned to the bedroom, Leanna was just hanging up.

"That was him," she said.

"Chubby?" Mangino asked behind the cup of coffee.

"Yep."

"So, how much he got?"

Leanna lit a cigarette. "Larry? Money?"

"Yeah, to both questions. How much? About how much?"

"A lot," Leanna said. "It's his mother's, though. Whatever he has is probably tied up. Except for these little bonuses he gets every few months. When he seems to have a lot of extra cash."

"To give away to barbers," Mangino said.

"He's always trying to impress his wimpy rich friends," she said. "He likes to feel connected. His father was supposed to be connected. Something like that. All those guys that come around, they all leech off him. His father is probably doing cartwheels in his grave."

"He gonna show up with the eighteen grand he's paying me to get his money back?" Mangino asked.

Leanna smiled. "You did something?" she asked. "What? To who? The barber?"

"Never mind," Mangino said. "Your boyfriend gonna have my money or not?"

"Tell me what you did first," Leanna said. "I like this. It's exciting. All Larry ever did was talk about doing something. You actually do do something."

Mangino seemed to think about it a few moments. "I gave the broad a facial," he said.

Leanna made a disgusted face. "She gave you a blow job?" she asked. "That Spanish woman? You let her touch you? Yuck."

Mangino returned the look. "I didn't say that."

Now Leanna looked confused. "Then what's a facial?"

"I knocked her teeth out," Mangino said.

"Oh!" Leanna said, smiling again. "Wow. Cool."

"So, he going to have my money or not?" Mangino asked Leanna one more time.

Leanna was standing naked in the bedroom doorway. A tuft of pink tissue paper was visible through her pubic hair. They had just finished another round of sex.

"Probably fifteen," Leanna said. "He has to feel like he out-smarted somebody. Then he'll brag to me how you're his new meat or something."

"Really?" Mangino asked.

Leanna walked to the bed and lay down on her stomach next to Mangino. She guided one of his hands to her legs. "Rub them, please?" she asked.

Mangino started to massage the backs of her legs. He rubbed them up and down a few times before he slapped her ass fairly hard.

"Ouch!" she said, turning her head toward him.

"You know how many of these I violated the last few years?" he asked her.

Leanna made a face. "That's disgusting," she said. "You're talking about men."

"You think it's any different, a fudge packing, between a man and a woman?"

Leanna was holding a hand up to him. "Please."

"We used condoms," he said.

"Yuck."

Mangino lit a cigarette. "So, you gonna help me take your boyfriend off?"

"I don't know," Leanna said. "What's in it for me? I stand a lot to lose."

"He's not marrying you, honey, trust me," Mangino said.

"And how would you know that?" Leanna asked.

"Because he made a point about calling you a cunt in front of me when you went to the bathroom the other night," Mangino said. Leanna's face tightened. "First he told me what a great piece of ass you are and then he said you were just another cunt."

Leanna was furious. She turned around and leaned on an elbow. "Are you fucking serious? That little-dick fat bastard called me that?"

Mangino made the sign of the cross. "Cross my heart and hope to die," he said. "The man doesn't appreciate your beauty."

Leanna was biting her lower lip. "Yeah, well, then fuck him," she said. "That motherfucking momma's boy piece of shit."

"Take it easy baby," Mangino said. "You can get even. You can get more than even."

"Yeah, tell me then," Leanna said. "What do you want me to do?"

"For now?" he said.

"What do I do!" Leanna yelled.

Mangino pointed to his eyes. "Like the coaches say, babe. Stay focused. For now, just stay focused."

Chapter 10

Aelish Phalen stood in the kitchen doorway and watched her boyfriend staring at the blank television screen. He had been sitting there the entire time she showered and dressed, since he had come home, more than forty minutes earlier.

Now she was wearing a short green skirt, a beige blouse and white high heels. She struggled clasping the pearl necklace behind her neck and stepped directly in front of Alex Pavlik's view. At first, he didn't even notice.

"Hello, love?" Aelish said.

"Huh?" Pavlik said. He looked up and his eyes opened wide. "Wow! You look good."

"Thank the lord," she said. "I was hoping for great but I was also starting to wonder if you weren't in a coma."

"I'm sorry," Pavlik said. "I had a bad day."

"You told me," Aelish said. "One of the bad guys did poo-poo in your cereal yesterday and you still aren't over it. But your new partner was right. You can't go around picking fights with people. Especially the bad guys. He probably saved you a lot of trouble."

"I've done it before," Pavlik said. "Gone at it with assholes like that."

"With Dexter there to back you," Aelish said. "He's not your partner anymore. You can't expect this new guy to just go along with something like that."

"This punk deserved it," Pavlik said. "He was Italian."

Aelish stared down at Pavlik until he smiled.

"What?" he asked. "He was. He's the same goon who scared the old man. I told you about that."

"Yes, and the day before that it was the goon who kicked a dog," Aelish said. "You can't run off and fight the world, man. Come to your senses already. Take it out on the punching bag at the gym."

"I'm trying here," Pavlik said. "It bothers me that I let him get to me, too. I know better. I don't know why it bothers me so much."

"Yes, well, normally this might be interesting, your tales of woe," Aelish said. She pointed at her watch. "But we have a dinner reservation on the boat leaving the West Side pier for eight-thirty."

Pavlik closed his eyes. "The New York Yacht thing," he said. "I'm sorry. I completely forgot."

"We have time," Aelish said. "If you take your shower and get dressed now and stop sulking over being bested in a test of big balls."

Pavlik was up and on his way to the bathroom. "I would've knocked the bum out," he said.

"I'm sure, love," Aelish said.

On the cruise, during a break between courses, they danced to the slow numbers. At the end of "Summer Wind," Aelish leaned into Pavlik and he kissed the back of her head.

"That was sweet," Aelish said.

"You smell delicious."

"Do you always kiss what smells delicious?"

"Always."

She pulled back to kiss him on the lips. "How was that?" she asked.

"I want to go home now," Pavlik said.

Aelish kissed him again.

"I think I might be falling for you," Pavlik said. A new slow dance started. They immediately stepped into it.

"Does that mean you're over it, the challenge of the penis thing," Aelish said.

"Huh? Oh, Christ, yeah. What made you think of that?"

"You caught me off guard, love."

"You're supposed to fall in step, though," Pavlik said. "You know, I say I'm falling for you, you say . . ."

"The Jets tickets!" she said.

"What?" Pavlik said. His face distorted.

"You were supposed to pick up the Jets tickets on the way in," Aelish said. "For your new partner."

Pavlik let go of her on the dance floor and just stared.

"What?" Aelish said, rubbing her arms. "I'm embarrassed."

Pavlik waved her to him. Aelish walked back into his arms and leaned her head against his right shoulder.

"I say I'm falling for you," he whispered. "And you say . . ."

Aelish smacked him in the right arm as she held him tight. "I already fell for you, you Lummox."

"Ouch," Pavlik said. "Oh."

John DeNafria watched his son playing a baseball game on the computer in the cramped living room of his one-bedroom apartment. Vincent DeNafria was thirteen years old but tall for his age. He had light blond hair and blue eyes.

DeNafria had his son until Vincent's mother returned from work. He had ordered pizza and soda for dinner. Vincent had been anxious to play on the computer from the time he walked into his father's apartment.

"Yeah!" Vincent yelled. "Piazza just hit number fifty."

"How many games left in the season?" DeNafria asked.

"Twenty-five," Vincent said. "And he's hitting three-fifty-two. That was his hundred and thirtieth RBI."

"In my day, Piazza would've hit twenty-five and been happy with that."

"He's great!" Vincent yelled.

"He's good," DeNafria replied. "Maybe very good. But they juice the ball and they moved all the fences in. It's a joke, the way these guys hit home runs today."

"Piazza hits monsters," Vincent said.

"Because they juice the ball," DeNafria said.

Vincent waved his father off.

"How 'bout you have a rain delay or something," DeNafria suggested. "Maybe spend half-an-hour with your old man tonight. You been here three hours and you played half a dozen games already."

Vincent typed at the keyboard and turned around on the chair. "Sorry, Dad," he said.

"It's alright," DeNafria said. "Of course, in my day, Strat-O-Matic was a game you could actually learn something with. Math, for instance. I didn't have a computer to do the ERA's and batting averages. None of the statistics were automatic."

"This is a lot easier, Dad," Vincent said.

"Tell me about it," DeNafria said. He handed his son a small plate of chocolate chip cookies. He set a glass of milk on the coffee table and sat back in his recliner.

"I can't drink that," Vincent said. "Not after the soda. I'll shit my brains out."

"Excuse me?" DeNafria said.

"Ask Mom," Vincent said. "Milk gives me the shits."

"Oh, child of mine, easy with the language, alright?"

Vincent shrugged. DeNafria lit a cigarette.

"How's your partner," Vincent asked. "Mom said you were getting a partner. You never had one before, right?"

"Not for a long time, no," DeNafria said. "He's alright. He was a boxer. Big guy. He used to fight in the ring."

"Can you take him?"

"I don't know. He's pretty big."

Vincent took a bite of cookie and spoke while he chewed. "What about your dating situation?"

DeNafria did a double take. "Huh?"

"Mom said I should ask you if you made me stop playing on the computer and wanted to talk to me," Vincent said.

"I see," DeNafria said. "What else she tell you to ask me?"

"Just that," Vincent said. "About your new partner and the dating thing. You really dating someone?"

"No," DeNafria said. "And your mother knows that already so I don't know why she told you to ask me."

Vincent shrugged again.

"What about you?" DeNafria asked his son. "At school? Any interested women?"

"No thanks," Vincent said. "I have enough trouble with

math."

"Which you wouldn't have if you played Strat-O-Matic the way it was meant to be played. Which is with the dice and a paper and pencil. Where you gotta do the math. Adding, subtracting, multiplying, division. You see what I'm saying?"

Vincent rolled his eyes. He said, "I don't have a girlfriend, Dad."

"Huh? Oh. Well, you will. Sooner than you think, too."

"I'd rather play baseball."

"You're smarter 'n me."

Vincent pointed at his father and smiled. "Because I use the computer."

DeNafria was caught off guard. "Huh? Oh, right," he said. "Eat a cookie."

Chapter 11

Larry Berra sat with Leanna at an outdoor table at Christina's, an Italian restaurant on Second Avenue. It was late afternoon but the sun was still hot. Most of the outdoor tables were occupied. Berra adjusted the umbrella to cover his bare shoulders from the sun. When he moved the umbrella, the sun caught Leanna flush in the eyes. She made a face and put on her sunglasses.

After a few minutes, Jimmy Mangino joined the couple. He noticed Leanna was wearing the teal tube top he had spotted in her dresser drawer a few nights earlier. Her chest was large under the cotton top.

The two men exchanged a cheek kiss then Mangino sat down across from Berra. He motioned toward Leanna. "It's alright to talk?" he asked.

Berra glanced at his girlfriend. She was sitting to his left. "Yeah, go 'head," he said.

Mangino glanced back at Leanna and smiled politely. "There was only twelve thousand in the envelope," he said. "The deal was for eighteen. I'm short six grand."

"The deal was for a body part," Berra said. He pointed at Mangino. "Your words."

Mangino fingered a cigarette. Berra reached across the table to light it for him. "All I got so far was a phone call and a promise for half the fifty-eight," Berra said. "It's not like I got the half. I can't see it. I can't count it. I didn't get a body part or money. If you're short, you think you're short, look at it from my perspective. I'm screwed."

Mangino grabbed a toothpick from a small vase. He pushed the wood through the plastic wrapper and sucked on the toothpick. "You got something more than you had last week," he said. "Respect. Did she mention what I did to them, her and her bartender?"

Berra nodded. "And she said she'd have to pay a lot in medical expenses. For herself and to keep his mouth shut. That that would have to come out of my end, too."

Mangino laughed. "She beats you for fifty-eight grand and you're supposed to pay for the doctor because you had to break somebody up to collect? What the fuck am I missing here?"

Leanna giggled to herself.

"You think this is funny?" Berra asked her.

Leanna tucked her head down. Her chin rested on the top of her right breast as she tried to suppress a laugh. She looked up and saw her boyfriend was still staring at her. "What?" she said.

"What's so fucking funny?" Berra asked.

"You," Leanna said. "That you pay for her bartender after they robbed you. I think that is hilarious."

Berra looked away from her. "The point being," he said to Mangino, "she has to pay for something else to keep the kid from going to the police."

"Oh, I can take care of that, him not going to the police," Mangino said. He was smiling at Leanna. "I'll tell her if you don't want to."

Berra saw his girlfriend smiling back at Mangino. "You having a good time?" he asked her.

Leanna rolled her eyes. "I have to go to the bathroom," she said. She stood up to leave.

Berra handed her a ten-dollar bill. "Get me a pack of Marlboro," he told her. "You want anything?" he asked Mangino.

Mangino waved off the offer.

"You sure you don't want me to pay?" Leanna asked Berra.

"Just get my fuckin cigarettes," Berra said.

Berra watched Leanna's ass as she headed up the short stairway to the sidewalk on Second Avenue. Mangino watched Berra.

"She's been on the rag since the other day," Berra said.

"Well, you were right," Mangino told Berra.

"About what?" Berra asked.

Mangino pointed toward the avenue. "Her."

Berra leaned back and sipped his wine. "How so?"

"She's a cunt," Mangino said. "Just like you said. She came on to me. I fucked her. I don't know if she bothered to tell you yet or not but I figured I would. Rather than watch you take that kind of abuse, like just now."

Berra was fumbling with his cigarette. "Are you fucking serious? You fucked her?"

"Yes," Mangino said. "I did. Same night I went to the restaurant. She asked me for my beeper the first night I met you. She made me write it on a napkin for her. She called me the next night. I didn't call back. She called me again the next day. She kept calling me. She doesn't respect you, Larry. She knows you won't marry her."

"How the fuck am I supposed to take this, what you're telling me here?" Berra asked.

"I'm doing you a favor," Mangino said. "I did you a favor. You know not to waste your time with her anymore. Or your money, which is all she was after. If you're insulted, if you think I slighted or dissed you, forget the rest of the eighteen. I can live with that. I'm looking to hook up with you, Larry. From where I sit, you're the man. You have the clout and the scratch to run things. I can be there for you. I'm interested in your money but only to the degree I can earn with you. I'm not looking to rob you or I would never have told you about her."

Berra downed the remainder of his wine. "I have to think about this," he said.

"Take your time," Mangino said. "You'll see I'm right once you think it over. I took her out of the picture before she could do any more damage, public or financial. She's a cunt. You don't need her."

Berra stood up. "I'm going home," he said.

Mangino nodded.

"Tell her not to bother calling when she comes back," Berra said.

Mangino nodded again. Berra left the bar somewhat shaky.

"You told him what?" Leanna yelled. "You stupid fuck!"

"It was to protect the game, kid, relax," Mangino said.

They were up in her apartment. Leanna was wearing the teal tube top and black thong panties. Mangino was still dressed except for his shirt. His chest and arm muscles were bulky and huge. He sipped at a beer as Leanna paced back and forth in front of him.

"Are you crazy?" she said. "You had to tell him that? Now?"

"To protect our investment, yeah," Mangino said.

"What investment? What game? I don't have anything going on with him. Nothing."

"But I do," Mangino said. "And I'm the one can sting him, not you. I'm the one can turn him over for a wad of cash. What have you gotten out of him so far. Maximum, I mean. What, five thousand? Ten thousand? I just beat him for twelve grand. I'll beat him for another ten at least by the end of the week. Maybe more."

"And what the fuck does that do for me?" Leanna said.

"Up front or down the road?" Mangino said. "You're not thinking."

Leanna stopped pacing. "Are you fucking serious? Do you think I'm half as stupid as Larry?"

"Not at all," Mangino said.

"Well, what did he say when you told him? Wasn't he upset? I mean, I was his girlfriend."

Mangino scratched at his chest hairs. "Larry is too scared to react that way," he said. "I think he was doing inventory the second I told him. What he has to gain versus what he has to lose. You know how that goes."

"The prick!" Leanna said. "I hate him! You should see his little dick. What a fucking loser."

Mangino got up off the couch and grabbed his shirt. "Why don't you shower or something," he said. "Take a bath and calm yourself down. I'll give you a call tomorrow. I have something going on in Brooklyn I'd like to bring you in on end of the week. It has something to do with Larry, too. Hooking him for some of the real cash he's holding onto."

Leanna put her hands on her hips. "What is it?"

"You'll see," Mangino said. "Go take that bath. Calm yourself down. I'm even too afraid to fuck you now, the way you are. Take a Valium, you got any. Calm down and I'll talk to you tomorrow."

"Fine," Leanna said. She held the apartment door open for Mangino to leave. She slammed it closed after him as soon as he was in the hall.

Chapter 12

They met at the Tiffany Diner in Bay Ridge, Brooklyn. DeNafria was wearing a blue NYFD sweatshirt and dungarees. Pavlik was dressed in a purple and gold Vikings sweat suit with a matching cap.

"How was your date?" DeNafria asked.

"Huh?" Pavlik said. He was taking a bite from a toasted bran muffin.

DeNafria stirred sugar into his coffee. "The boat thing?"

"Oh, nice. It was nice. I highly recommend it."

"I might go except she left me."

"Oh, right. Sorry."

DeNafria moved the remainder of the scrambled eggs on his plate around with his fork.

"They found a body in Canarsie this morning," Pavlik said. "I don't know if it means anything but a friend told me it looks like a mob thing. The feds were there almost immediately after it was called in."

DeNafria sipped his coffee. "I'm listening."

"My ex-partner, Dexter Greene, called me this morning," Pavlik continued. "He's still with homicide. He lives in Canarsie. The guy was shot six times. Twice in the head. Dex didn't know anything about him, but he said they found all kinds of porno shit at the guy's apartment."

DeNafria sipped ice water from a blue plastic cup. "Can your ex find anything else out for us?" he asked. "Without having to reach out, I mean."

"He called me because it had to do with porn," Pavlik said. "It was an alert more than a tip."

"I'm sure we'll hear about it sooner or later," DeNafria said. "We need to stop in and find out what Ms. Gonzalez is doing for us. I'll lay five to one the tape machine isn't even hooked up."

"What about you?" Pavlik said. "Hear anything?"

"If you count lost dogs," DeNafria said. "Tony Pug put out a five grand reward for his dog. Apparently somebody stole it."

Pavlik was reading DeNafria's eyes. "Five grand is a lot of money," he said.

DeNafria wasn't paying attention. "These guys are all nuts," he said. "Pay five grand for a dog one day and break a guy's arm for being fifty dollars short on some bullshit baseball bet another day."

Pavlik stopped short of taking a drink of milk from a glass. "Oh, I have something for you and your kid," he said. He pulled two tickets from his sweat suit jacket pocket. "Jets and the Bills, November 8."

DeNafria was impressed. "Wow!" he said. "Thanks. This is great."

"Forty yard line. Tenth row. Jets sideline."

"That's great. How much do I owe—"

Pavlik waved it off. "Forget it."

"No, serious. I don't know I can return the favor. How much?"

"Forget it. Enjoy the game with your kid."

DeNafria stashed the tickets inside his wallet. "We will," he said. "Thanks again. Vincent will be forever in your debt. He already wants your autograph. I told him you were a boxer."

"I wasn't a very good one. Not professionally. I usually lost."

"He'll tell his friends you were the heavyweight champion."

"Great."

"Vincent's a good kid. He's going through it right now, though. Me and his mom and all."

"Who's he named after?"

"My father."

"Guinea tradition, right?"

"It's an Italian thing, yeah."

Pavlik raised both his hands. "It was another joke," he said. DeNafria raised his hands. "No problem."

Pavlik spread jelly on the remaining half of his muffin. "How did you make out with the barber's girlfriend?" he asked.

"She's running a game," DeNafria said. He was spooning lemon pits out of his tomato juice. "Big time game. Vittorio isn't the only sucker on her list. Who knows how many suckers she has forking over money to that restaurant."

Pavlik scratched his head. "How do guys do that, mortgage their houses like that?"

"Amore," DeNafria said.

"Amore my ass. The guy is sixty-something years old. How stupid is that? You really don't think she'll help, huh?"

"I doubt it. If she doesn't talk to her lawyer first, maybe. I wouldn't count on it, though. She's been around the block a few times, Ms. Gonzalez. She knows the ropes."

"What about Larry Berra's goons? What if they talk to her, too?"

"They're definitely competition. Except like I said, Lucia isn't a naive woman. She's a street-smart broad. She may have her own security in place. At least for the first round of threats."

"You think?"

"Enough to scare off old men, at least."

"Why don't we approach her," Pavlik said. "I have nothing scheduled the rest of the afternoon. I'll be in her neighborhood anyway. My gym is a few blocks from the place. Can you meet me?"

"Yeah, sure," DeNafria said. "I'm curious whether or not they approached her yet. Like I said, I doubt the recorder I installed is even plugged in."

"Good enough," Pavlik said. He took a large bite from the bran muffin. "I won't identify myself. Maybe it'll convince her to hook up the machine."

DeNafria made a face at Pavlik's sweat suit. "I thought you didn't like football," he said.

"I got it as a present," Pavlik said. "As a goof."

"It looks real."

"It is. I arrested one of the players from the Vikings a few years back the night before a game. Drunk and disorderly. My partner talked me into letting the guy off the hook. The guy sent me this in the mail a few weeks later. Actually, it was his agent sent it to my partner in the mail."

"That takes balls, wearing your graft," DeNafria said.

Pavlik pointed at DeNafria. "It's the same guy with the Jets tickets," he said.

The waiter at TAPAZ, TAPAZ, TAPAZ was busy writing the Specials menu on the portable blackboard when detectives

DeNafria and Pavlik arrived at the restaurant. Pavlik flashed his badge while DeNafria walked deeper inside the restaurant to look for Lucia Gonzalez.

"She's in the hospital," the waiter said. He was a tall thin Hispanic man with a dark complexion and a thin mustache. "She won't be back for another week at least she says. She was mugged."

"Where's the bartender?" DeNafria asked as he returned to the front of the restaurant. "The kid was here the other day."

The waiter thumbed toward the door. "He was mugged, too," he said. He held his chin. "Broken jaw."

"You see it?" Pavlik asked. "Here? It happened here?"

The waiter shrugged. "All I know is they say they were mugged. There was blood here in the restaurant, on one of the tables, on the floor, but they said they were mugged, that's all."

The detectives looked at each other.

"Mangino," DeNafria said.

Pavlik's jaw tightened. He spoke to the waiter. "Nobody saw anything? She isn't pressing charges?"

"She said she didn't want to get mugged again," the waiter said. "She's not calling the cops."

"Do you have a telephone number where I can reach her?" DeNafria asked.

The waiter held both his hands up. "She told me not to give out her number, man. I'm sorry. She's my boss. I can't afford to lose my job."

"I'm a cop," DeNafria said. "This is police business."

"The police going to employee me, man?" the waiter asked. "No way. I'm not giving nobody any numbers."

DeNafria stared the waiter down. Pavlik went to the telephone to check on the recording device. He looked around the phone for the connecting wire but it wasn't there.

"Anything?" DeNafria asked while he continued to stare at the waiter.

"It's not here," Pavlik said.

"You know where she put it?" DeNafria asked the waiter. "I installed a recorder the other night."

"It was in a box under the counter," the waiter said. His voice was less antagonistic now. "I don't know if it's still there."

Pavlik looked under the counter but didn't see anything. He searched on his knees under the bar sinks. He found two plastic milk crates. One was filled with dirty wet rags. The other contained several bottles of cleaning liquid. "It isn't here," he said.

"The busboys cleaned the place up," the waiter said. "They probably moved it, if it was there."

Pavlik was up off the floor. "We'll take that number now," he told the waiter.

The waiter held up both his hands again. "Can't do," he said. "I'm sorry, man, but she'll fire my ass."

Pavlik pulled a set of handcuffs out of his back pocket. He cracked one open on the waiter's right wrist.

"What the fuck?" the waiter said. He stepped back before Pavlik could cuff the other wrist.

"The phone number or you're under arrest for stealing police property," Pavlik said.

"You can't do that," the waiter said. "I didn't steal shit, man." He turned to DeNafria.

Pavlik folded his arms across his chest and waited. "You're probably right," he told the waiter. "The charge won't stick but I guarantee you'll spend the night in lockup before we release you."

The waiter was panicked. He looked from Pavlik to DeNafria and back. "He can't do that," he said. "You can't do that."

Pavlik stepped toward the waiter. "Watch me," he said.

"Alright, alright," the waiter said. "I'll give you the fuckin number, man. Let me go."

Pavlik winked at DeNafria. "Sure," he said. "No problem, buddy."

Chapter 13

Mangino and Luchessi talked in a stairwell at Madison Square Garden at the half of a New York Knicks and Miami Heat basketball game. Mangino sipped beer from a tall container. Luchessi spread mustard from a plastic packet onto a foot-long frankfurter.

"These motherfuckers," Luchessi said. "I should've known better than to lay anything against Miami."

"Tell me about it," Mangino said. "This fuckin convict, Sprewell, he took the wrong night off."

"That's the problem," Luchessi said as he took a bite from the frankfurter. "He was never convicted. They never even arrested him. The NBA gave him a year off, some kickback on his paycheck, and these assholes signed him for whatever the fuck it is, a hundred million. Imagine, a hundred million to shoot a fuckin basketball?"

"And they can't even do that," Mangino said.

Luchessi swallowed some frankfurter and immediately took another bite. He swallowed the second bite and held a finger up at Mangino. "Actually," he said, "you ever hear this kid talk? Sprewell, I mean. He's an articulate bone. And he's pretty consistent as far as performance. Fifteen, twenty, twenty-two points a game. And he hustles. Except he takes his time getting to practice, some lateness thing, he's been the Knicks most consistent player."

"Except for tonight," Mangino said.

Luchessi took another bite from the frankfurter and continued his thought. "Then there's the kid in Philadelphia, the one with all the tattoos, 'The Answer' he calls himself. ESPN claims he shows up forty-five minutes late for practice. Chronic lateness they called it. He should get himself another tattoo, 'The Problem.' Imagine showing to work forty-five minutes late every day? How long you think you'd have that job?"

"Which is one reason I don't work," Mangino said. "Although you expect it from these clowns. Ten–twenty million a year and they don't show for practice. No wonder they don't show for the games either. At least not the nights I bet them."

Both men stopped to eat and drink.

"You work out something with Larry Berra?" Luchessi asked as he chewed on his food.

"I got something in mind," Mangino said.

Luchessi was still chewing. "You want to share it?"

"I was gonna surprise you," Mangino said. "I got the idea from Eugene."

"Tranchatta?" Luchessi asked.

"The same."

"What the fuck is it, a drug deal?"

"Better than that," Mangino said. "Let me surprise you, you'll like it."

Luchessi pointed a finger from behind the remainder of the frankfurter he was holding. "So long's you don't blow it," he said.

Both men checked their watches.

"Speaking of Eugene," Luchessi said. "Try to pin him down. We shouldn't give him too much time to maneuver."

"I'll be seeing him again tomorrow," Mangino said.

Luchessi finished the frankfurter. He wiped his mouth with the paper napkin and tossed it down the stairs. "You see his broad?" he asked Mangino. "Larry's girlfriend."

Mangino smiled. "Sure did," he said.

"Somethin' else, huh?"

"She's a pretty girl."

Luchessi guided Mangino back out to the hallway. "At least he did something right with his mother's money, the dumb fuck."

"I guess," Mangino said.

His older brother, Giovanni, had given him the gun five years earlier, after the liquor store he had owned was robbed for the last time. Vittorio Tangorra's sister-in-law had been killed in the robbery. Giovanni Tangorra had never had the chance to defend himself or his wife that day. They had kept the gun inside the cash register. When the thieves came, Giovanni had been in the bathroom. He was cleaning himself when he heard the shots. When he came out, his wife lay dying in a pool of blood. She had been shot three times in the neck.

Giovanni had given his younger brother the gun the same day he buried his wife. He lived the next year in futile loneliness and finally took his own life—less than a year after his wife was murdered.

Now Vittorio Tangorra was carrying the same .25mm with him everywhere. When he stepped out of the barbershop for a cigarette break, he saw Larry Berra waving to him from across Twenty-third Street. Tangorra slid his right hand inside his front pants pocket and touched the handle of the gun.

Berra was dressed in a dark business suit. He carried a black leather briefcase. He set the briefcase down between his legs and waited for Tangorra on the south sidewalk. Tangorra glanced back at the barbershop as he started across the street. Berra was smiling. He held both hands up over his head.

"No trouble!" Berra yelled. "I just want to talk."

"What you want?" Tangorra asked.

"To make a deal," Berra said.

The barber was skeptical. He kept a few feet of distance between them. "I don't got the money," he said. "I told you that. I don't got fifty thousand dollar."

Berra finally lowered his hands. "It's closer to sixty but I don't care about that," he said. He grabbed his briefcase with one hand and offered his free hand to the old man.

Tangorra ignored the gesture. "You smack me like child," he said. "I don't forget that."

"I'm sorry about that," Berra said. "I lost my temper."

"You half my age," Tangorra said. "You hit me like child. Throw me on the floor."

"I'm sorry."

"I don't pay you."

"Trust me, I know."

"What you want?"

"Help."

"What kind of help?"

"With the police. I need you to help me with the police."

"They come to my house," Tangorra said. "Detective."

Berra nodded. "I understand."

"They want you to talk to me on the phone."

Berra waved his hands. "I'm not looking for the money anymore, Vittorio. I just want some help."

"How am I know you want help? I'm old man. What can I do for you?"

"I need you to talk to the detective for me," Berra said. "Talk to the detective and we forget the money. That fair enough?"

Tangorra pulled out his wallet. He fingered through a small pack of cards and pulled the card Detective John DeNafria had given him. "You have pen?" Tangorra asked Berra.

Berra was pulling a pen from his inside jacket pocket. "Sure," he said. "Right here."

Mangino watched the transaction from a hole in the closet door. Tranchatta and a well-dressed middle-aged Russian man exchanged packages at the back desk of the office. Tranchatta counted several stacks of hundred-dollar bills while the Russian tested cocaine from a plastic bag. When the Russian finished testing the product, he taped the plastic bag and slipped it inside his sports jacket pocket. He shook Tranchatta's hand and waited for Tranchatta to stash the cash in a desk drawer.

Tranchatta then followed the Russian out of the office to the parking lot. There he shook the Russian's hand one more time before turning back for the office.

Now Mangino was watching Tranchatta on the security screen on the last desk in the office. He waited for Tranchatta to enter the office before putting his feet up on the back desk.

"That was easy enough," he said.

"I just hope it never ends," Tranchatta said. "This guy is good for two-three deliveries a month. I almost get nervous now when he wants more. You know what I mean? That thing about greed being the great downfall. I'm afraid they'll catch on to him and that'll be the end of it."

Mangino took a long drag on his cigarette and pointed at the drawers. "I couldn't see," he said. "Which one was it?"

Tranchatta laughed the question off. "Were you at least packing?" he asked. He thumbed over his shoulder. "I just assume these guys dealing this stuff are carrying guns."

Mangino showed Tranchatta the .9mm Beretta he had strapped in an ankle holster. He pointed to the drawers again. "Which one was it?" he asked again.

"You're in a rush, huh?" Tranchatta said. He waved at Mangino to move his feet off the desk. "Here, let me at it," he said.

Mangino pushed his chair back away from the desk as Tranchatta used a key to unlock the drawer where he had put the cash. Tranchatta then sat on the desk, his back to the office door, and counted the money. Mangino watched him the entire time.

When Tranchatta finished counting the money, he separated two stacks and counted five hundred-dollar bills from one of the stacks.

"Five bills," he said. He handed the cash to Mangino. "Like you said, that was easy enough, right?"

Mangino frowned at the money in his hand. He pointed to the two stacks of cash on the desk. "What about that?" he asked.

"One is the cost for the product and the other is my half, you don't mind," Tranchatta said. "You complaining about a five hundred dollar score?"

"You didn't mention the cost," Mangino said.

"I didn't think I had to," Tranchatta said. "You don't think I got that stuff for free, I hope."

Mangino pointed at the money again. "Which stack is yours?"

"Huh?"

"How much did you get it for?"

Tranchatta looked back at the money and waved his hands. "What are you getting at, Jimmy?"

"What it cost?" Mangino asked again.

Tranchatta made a face. "You aren't serious, are you?"

"Sure I am."

"This was a favor I did for you, Jimmy," Tranchatta said. He stood with his arms out. "I mean, what the fuck here."

Mangino eyed the cash on the desk. "How much did the fuckin product cost?" he asked one more time.

Tranchatta tried his best to stand his ground. "None of your fuckin business," he said.

"Really?" Mangino said.

Tranchatta went to grab the cash off the desk and Mangino was up out of the chair. He grabbed Tranchatta's right hand in a vice grip. He fished a lighter from his pants pocket and lit the flame. He held the flame under Tranchatta's right wrist until the room was filled with a loud throaty scream.

Mangino held the flame to Tranchatta's wrist until the skin turned black. He let go and Tranchatta fell to the floor. He rolled to one side and held onto his burned wrist with his free hand. He moaned from the pain as he rocked on his side.

"Now," Mangino said. "How much did it cost?"

Chapter 14

"Who's this guy again?" Pavlik asked his partner.

They were watching a dark complexioned man in his mid-twenties jogging east along Shore Road in Brooklyn. The detectives were parked in DeNafria's minivan off the corner of Ninety-first Street and Shore Road. All of the windows in the minivan were tinted black. Pavlik watched the jogger through a small pair of opera glasses.

"Jack Fama," DeNafria said. "He's on Joe Sharpetti's crew in Coney Island. He's an off-the-boat nephew of Aniello Vignieri, from the other side. Slick-looking stud some of the wiseguy women can't keep their hands off."

Pavlik focused on the jogger's face. "He's cute but I wouldn't call him a stud. He made?"

DeNafria was looking through his notebook. "A couple years ago," he said. "Him and five other guys around his age. The mob is getting desperate."

Pavlik was squinting. "Why's that name so familiar to me? Sharpetti, I mean."

DeNafria turned to a page in his notebook labeled: JOE SHARP (SHARPETTI) and handed it to Pavlik.

Pavlik started reading the names top to bottom:

Phil ("Philly Lights") Cuccia (Made, 1/85)

Johnny ("Cards") Cuccia (Made, 6/90)

Joey ("Joe Quack") Quastifarro (Made, 6/90)

Louie ("Big Louie") Telese (Made, 1/85)

Nicholas ("NG"/"No Good") Galafini (Made, 1/88)

Bobby ("Feet") DeMarco (Made, 1/88)

~~Johnny ("the knife") Sessa (Made, 6/90)~~

Jack ("Jackie Slick") Fama (Made, 6/98)

"What's with the lines through the name?" Pavlik asked.

"Sessa?" DeNafria asked. "He's dead."

Pavlik glanced at DeNafria with a smirk. "Natural or otherwise?"

"Otherwise," DeNafria said. "Two in the head. I didn't bother to mark it because he was already dead when I started this notebook."

Pavlik continued to read the names on the list:

Francis ("Frankie Fruits") Torturro (Associate)

Jimmy ("Jimmy Calamari") Pinto (Associate)

Joey ("Joey Fish") Pesci (Associate)

Greg Scarpella (Associate)

Michael Scarpella (Associate)

~~Eddie Senta (Associate)~~

"I know this guy!" Pavlik said. "Why's the line through his name? He get killed?"

DeNafria leaned to his right to see the book. "Eddie Senta? He did some time and retired. Really retired. He wasn't a made guy so they let him cut loose. Left it all behind for the straight and narrow. He was close to Joe Sharp."

"Tell me about it," Pavlik said. "We had a case involving him and some guy the feds were letting run loose. I was in Senta's house during a shootout there. His kid was clipped in the leg. His wife and kid were hostages."

DeNafria shook his head. "I know most of these guys are scumbags, but how the hell do they let their families get involved in this shit?"

"No, no," Pavlik said as he handed the notebook back to DeNafria. "It was nothing like that. The guy ran into a room with gunfire. He killed one of the bad guys, a Russian mobster. I swore this guy Senta was the killer until I was there and saw for myself. It was back a little more than a year ago, the thing on the Upper East Side in Manhattan. Me and my partner took the call. Three people whacked in an apartment up there. Turned out the killer was in the witness protection program, God bless the federal government. This Senta was somehow caught in the middle of the shit. He was clean, though. At least in that thing, he was."

"Whatever," DeNafria said. "This guy, Fama, he's on his way for wiseguy nookie, right now. Two blocks up. Rosemary DiCicco of 'Ronnie-boy' DiCicco fame. A skipper, no less."

Pavlik was squinting. "I thought that was against the rules?"

"Please," DeNafria said. "That's the first thing you'll notice you're working O.C. long enough. None of the rules apply unless you're high up enough to dictate them down. Even then, sooner or later, the rules get changed on the fly." He fingered a piece of chocolate Kit-Kat bar from an open pack on the console. "Anyway, this kid was made a couple years ago. He's porking at least two wives of fellow wiseguys we know of. DiCicco is up in Elmira.

Fama makes his stops here at least twice a week. Mrs. DiCicco is quite the looker."

"That what we're doing here, P.I. work for her husband?" Pavlik asked.

DeNafria pointed at Fama jogging further up the street. "Fama, since he came here, was a close friend of Mangino," he said. "A very close friend. If anybody knows where Mangino is sleeping nights, he does. Jimmy hasn't been using his apartment the last week. He's been out late nights and not coming home. His family, what's left of the ones who talk to him, are out in Jersey someplace. I want to head out to Jersey later and talk to Ms. Gonzalez about her recent injuries. In the meantime, I also want to find out where Mangino is hiding. In case we want to question him."

"I'd like to do more than question him," Pavlik said.

DeNafria stretched his arms over his head. "If I can convince the woman to press charges, you may get the chance," he said through a yawn.

"Don't be so enthusiastic about it," Pavlik said.

"I'm not," DeNafria said.

"He fuck you this morning already?" Jack Fama asked Rosemary DiCicco.

At forty-two, Mrs. DiCicco was still an attractive woman. She was a tall busty blond with pale smooth skin, long hair and bright blue eyes. She was wearing an open crimson satin robe and white slippers. Both her breasts were exposed.

She glanced at her watch. "Before he took a shower," she said. Her voice was tired.

Fama made a face.

"But it's almost noon already," Mrs. DiCicco noticed. She sucked on a fresh cigarette and left a lipstick stain on the filter. "I was just getting dressed when I heard the bell," she added.

Fama rubbed his face in aggravation. He was a dark-skinned Sicilian with dark brown eyes and a muscular build. "Goddamn shit," he said with a touch of an Italian accent. "I want to eat pussy for breakfast. Now I have to wait."

Mrs. DiCicco pointed upstairs. "I have another shower upstairs," she said. "I'll be clean in ten minutes."

Fama made a face. "I don't eat what other man fucks, please," he said. He pointed to the stairway further back in the hallway. "Go upstairs and shower. You can blow me later."

Mrs. DiCicco was yawning. "Gee, thanks," she said with sarcasm. "I can hardly wait."

"Go," Fama said. "I'm busy with Jimmy now." He tapped her on the ass through the robe as he slipped by her in the hallway.

"There are rules against fucking wiseguy wives," Fama told Jimmy Mangino.

They were in the basement apartment of the house. Mangino was putting on his socks. He was naked except for the black underwear he was wearing.

"That broad," Mangino said. "She runs on fucking batteries. I couldn't turn her off."

Fama was smiling. "She's good, though, Jimmy. Yes or no? I come here sometimes two-three time a week."

Mangino yawned. "You're in better shape than I am. I haven't worked out ten times since I'm out."

Fama took a seat on the second from last step in the basement. "You want to move out, just say so," he said. "I can put you on a boat in Mill Basin or Howard Beach. It's where they'll make you once this is over. On one of the boats."

"Gimme another day or two here," Mangino said. "It's convenient, running around from here. There's only two roads can get you into Mill Basin."

"No problem," Fama said. He waited a few minutes while Mangino finished getting dressed.

Mangino zipped up his dungarees and pointed over Fama's head up the stairs. "You sure I'm gonna be alright, this guy, her husband, when he gets out? I know you're protected, being a blood relative and all, but I'm just another guy."

Fama waved it off. "He's not getting out for another seven years," he said. "Without somebody else doesn't give him up and they add even more time."

"What about word gets around, though?" Mangino asked.

"So, you compare notes," Fama said. "You think we the only two fucking this woman? Please."

"Why's she like this? So easy and all?"

"She was a dancer when Ronnie meet her," Fama said. Mangino made a face of disbelief. "That is what I am told," Fama said. "So, you shouldn't marry her," he said. "She is *putana*, eh? She can't be faithful. She can't help herself."

Mangino fished a shoebox from under the bed. He set it on the bed and opened the top. "Take your pick," he said as he removed the top of the box.

Four different handguns were inside the shoebox. Fama pointed to one of them. "The three-eighty," he said.

Mangino removed a Browning .380mm and a .9mm Beretta from the shoebox. He handed Fama the .380mm and jammed the .9mm inside the waist of his dungarees.

"You sure these Koreans will show?" Fama asked. "I don't like to carry all this if they don't."

Mangino held up a finger. "According to Eugene," he said. "They're supposed to have cocaine and a lot of it. We'll see. As for a time, who knows? In the meantime, I got two other appointments today I need to make myself."

"I have one I can't miss," Fama said. He stroked the air with a fist. "Joe Sharp's weekly blow job meeting. We have to walk on the fucking boardwalk so the FBI can't tape our conversations. Joe Sharp makes you lean over and talk in whisper in his ear. He don't always clean his ear. Yucky-filthy they are sometimes."

"Translation, you won't be around later," Mangino said. "You're out."

Fama shrugged. "Not until late," he said.

"Then I'll kill the bald fuck myself," Mangino said. "What about the barber? Can you go see him?"

Fama raised his eyebrows. "Excuse me, who's the made guy here?"

Mangino was on his way up the stairs. "Right," he said. "Can you go see the barber, big shot?"

"I thought these guys aren't supposed to cross crews," Pavlik said.

"There isn't a rule these guys don't break," DeNafria said.

They had moved the minivan a few hundred feet from the house. They watched Jimmy Mangino and Jack Fama exit the large brick house. The two mobsters used a red Trans Am parked across the street from the house.

"Isn't Sharpetti gambling and loans?" Pavlik asked.

"The more respectable trades," DeNafria said. "Yeah." He took down the Trans Am license number.

"Don't we get to see the woman?" Pavlik asked.

"Mrs. DiCicco?"

"Yeah," Pavlik said. "I never seen a mob wife. Not up close."

The Trans Am made a quick U-turn in the street and headed away from them. It turned left at the far corner. Pavlik opened the door and was out of the Minivan before DeNafria could stop him. He walked up to the house and rang the doorbell several times.

"I'm coming!" he heard a woman yell from inside.

He removed his wallet and opened it so his badge was showing. Rosemary DiCicco opened the door without asking who it was. She was wearing a white workout bra and red thong panties.

Pavlik smiled politely. "Good morning," he said.

Mrs. DiCicco saw the badge and immediately frowned. "Morning has long come and gone," she said.

"You mean those aren't your jammies?" Pavlik asked.

Mrs. DiCicco flipped him the bird. "What do you want?"

"Police," Pavlik said.

"Yeah, that's why you have a badge," Mrs. DiCicco said without flinching. She defiantly placed both her hands on her hips.

Pavlik stuttered from looking down at her legs. "Ah, is James Mangino here, ma'am?"

"No, he's not."

"Do you know where he is?"

"Nope."

"Was he here earlier?"

"Nope."

"You sure, ma'am?"

"Yep."

Pavlik held his chin. "Hmmm," he said. His eyes wondered to Mrs. DiCicco's legs.

"Here, I'll make it easier for you," she said. She turned around and let Pavlik see her ass. "Okay?"

"Fine, ma'am," Pavlik said.

"You got your thrill?"

"Yes, ma'am."

Mrs. DiCicco forced a phony smile. "Then have a nice day," she said before slamming the front door in his face.

"Right," Pavlik said. "Thank you."

Chapter 15

She remembered seeing the man with the salt and pepper hair and the FBI shirt in her gym on Tuesday and Thursday mornings. Usually, the man attended the spinning class. Leanna wore her tight white spandex shorts. A tight fitted gray halter hugged her breasts. Her hair was tied up with a white scrunchie.

She waited for the man where she had noticed he worked with light arm weights after the cycling class. When he started pumping his biceps with twenty-five pound dumbbells, Leanna positioned herself on the edge of a nearby bench and called to him.

"Excuse me, Mr. FBI man," she said. "Can you help me a second when you're finished."

The man with the FBI T-shirt set the dumbbells on the rubber-matted floor.

"What do you need?" he asked.

Leanna pointed to a twenty-pound dumbbell in a rack in front of the long wall-mirror. "That," she said. "Can you hand it to me over my head?"

"Sure," the man said.

"Thank you."

Leanna took her position and waited for the man to hand her the dumbbell. "Can you help me when I'm done?" she asked.

The man smiled. "Of course."

Leanna quickly completed eight repetitions and handed the weight back to the man. "Thanks a lot," she said.

"No problem," the man said. He set the weight back in the rack.

"I love your shirt," Leanna told him. "Are you really an FBI man?"

"My name is George," the man said. He extended his right hand to her.

Leanna took his hand and favored the man with a wink. "In my fantasy, you're just the FBI man."

George smiled. "FBI man works for me, too," he said.

Half-an-hour later, George and Leanna were sipping orange juice drinks under an umbrella at a coffee shop on Second Avenue. George was still dressed in his sweaty workout clothes. Leanna was wearing a white nylon Nike sweat suit.

Leanna explained her situation with the men in her life. George explained a situation with a wife.

"So, you're interested in me, but only for sex," Leanna said.

George stretched his arms back and yawned. "Dinners, drinks, an occasional weekend thing maybe," he said.

"I see," Leanna said. "At least you're a straight shooter."

"And you're interested in me because of this situation with a gangster and a wannabe boyfriend," George said. "Or is that part of the fantasy, too?"

"Are you really FBI?" Leanna asked. "I know you can buy those T-shirts anywhere."

"But why would you want to wear one?" George said. He dug in his gym bag for his wallet and flipped it open to show his identification badge. He kept his thumb across his last name.

"It looks official," Leanna said.

"I'm not supposed to get involved with people who require the agency's help," George said playfully. "You can understand that."

"But couldn't I just look at an FBI photo book and pick you out?" Leanna asked coltishly. "I mean, if I really wanted to?"

"I guess," George said. "But you'd have to go through some effort for that."

"I could get your last name from the gym, George," Leanna said, waving him off.

George handed Leanna his identification badge. She read from it.

"Special agent, George Wilson," Leanna read. "The Federal Bureau of Investigation."

"What would you like me to do for you, Leanna?" George asked.

"Hang around," Leanna said. "I don't know what's going on with Larry and Jimmy but I know I don't want anything to do with it. Hang around so I can back them off if I have to."

"I can't follow you," George said.

"Just give me your card," she said. "And tell me that if I call, you'll come running. Or your friends at the Bureau will come running. Larry is a creampuff but this Jimmy guy is dangerous. He's already beat up one woman."

"Do you want to file a complaint now?" George asked. "I can bring you to the police and get things rolling much faster than if you did it without me. This Jimmy would know to back off if we did that."

Leanna let out a deep breath. "No, not yet," she said. "I don't want to antagonize him either. He may just do whatever he intends to do and leave me out of it. No, not yet. But I'll keep it in mind."

"Fine," George said. "Whatever you say."

Leanna squinted at George. "I say it's time we fuck, George," she said.

"Your place or mine?" George said.

"I thought you were married," Leanna said.

"I was," George said.

John DeNafria questioned Lucia Gonzalez at her apartment in North Bergen, New Jersey. She lived on the second floor of a three-family house off Kennedy Boulevard. The neighborhood was mostly middle-class Cuban-Hispanic. The houses were well kept.

Lucia was sitting up in a recliner in her living room. A glass of water, several bottles of prescription pills and some cotton gauze were set on a metal snack tray to the left of the recliner. Lucia could barely open her mouth. She had fifty-two stitches and three missing teeth.

"We never found the tape recorder," DeNafria told Lucia.

"Please," she managed to say.

"Was it a guy named Jimmy Mangino?" he asked.

Lucia closed her eyes.

DeNafria laid out a set of mug shots. Pictures of Jimmy Mangino and Larry Berra were among them. "Was Larry there?" he asked.

Lucia shook her head.

"Just Mangino?" DeNafria asked. He pointed to the picture of Mangino. "Him?"

Lucia tried to frown but it was too painful. "I don't know," she said. "I don't know him."

"You can't let them get away with this," DeNafria said. "I can put him away for this. For a few years if you cooperate. He's a bad guy, Lucia. He'll come back if you don't put him away. He's an animal."

"I'm not doing anything," she managed to say. "Nothing."

DeNafria scratched at the back of his head. "What about your bartender? Is he willing to talk?"

"I doubt it," Lucia said.

"He's your boyfriend, right?"

"He's a friend."

"Is he here?"

Lucia shook her head again. "No."

"He wasn't home," DeNafria said. "I stopped there on my way here."

"He went to P.R.," Lucia said.

DeNafria made a face. "Puerto Rico?"

Lucia nodded.

"Great," DeNafria said. "Thanks a lot."

Chapter 16

Dexter Greene was sitting in his recliner in the den of his house watching a VCR tape of the black production of Bizet's Carmen, *Carmen Jones,* when Alex Pavlik arrived with a calzone. Greene was dressed in gray sweatpants and a white T-shirt. Pavlik was in a black turtleneck, gray slacks, and a black blazer. He set the calzone on the coffee table and stopped to look at the television. Harry Belafonte was singing to Dorothy Dandridge.

"Christ," Pavlik said just before he dropped onto the couch.

Greene scowled as he reached for the remote.

Pavlik said, "What ever happened to Day-O, Day-O, Day-O?"

Greene shut the VCR off. "Aelish kicked you out already?"

"Nope," Pavlik said. "I stopped by to visit a friend."

"You mean haunt one," Greene said.

"No, I meant stop by to see one," Pavlik said. "He wasn't home so I came here to see you instead." He pointed to the bag on the coffee table. "The calzone is probably cold."

Greene turned in the recliner to face Pavlik. "I don't suppose you recognize the music."

"*Carmen,*" Pavlik said. "You gonna open that or should I?" He was pointing to the bag again.

"How the fuck you know that?" Greene asked.

"I took a course," Pavlik said. He gave up waiting for Greene and opened the bag himself.

"Took a course, my ass," Greene said.

"Really," Pavlik said. "In college." He had removed the aluminum foil from one end of the calzone. "You think I could get a plate here?"

"Fuck you," Greene said. "Use the napkins. What course in what college?"

Pavlik pulled off a corner of the calzone and immediately took a bite. He spoke while he chewed. "An opera course at Albany," he said. "It was an elective and I thought I might meet some broads with class."

Greene made a face. "Who's the composer?"

"Bizet," Pavlik said.

"How come you never mentioned this before? Eight years we were together, I'm just finding this out now."

"Lighten up, bro. What's the big deal? You never asked before."

"I didn't ask this time."

Pavlik took a second bite of the calzone. "Yes, you did."

Greene was squinting. "What you come here for?"

"Break your balls," Pavlik said. "The guy killed in Canarsie. What's up with that? That how you people say it?"

"He was a fag," Greene said. "Something to do with porn. The FBI took control of the investigation as soon as the crime scene was established. Off the record, it was mob related. The fag was involved with the Vignieri family somehow. Probably the guys they found off the pier here a few weeks ago. The word is, the

Vignieri's are cleaning up."

"According to the Jerry Capeci article they are," Pavlik said. "What else you hear?"

"You're the one in O.C.," Greene said. "What the hell you do all day, sign autographs?"

"I'm outside the loop," Pavlik said. He reached down to pull off another piece of the calzone. "Gimme some names at least. I have to meet my new partner later and I want to impress him."

"What names?" Greene said. "I'm homicide, remember? Special cases. I got a promotion too but it didn't get the press attention your lucky-ass bust did. I thank the white media for that, don't kid yourself."

"Jealousy will get you nowhere, Dex," Pavlik said.

Greene flipped Pavlik the finger. "The only name I heard was the generic Vignieri name," he said. "Nobody in particular. The guy had something to do with their porn operation, whoever was running it for them. He probably got capped because they found him. The apartment was an illegal. He was probably hiding."

Pavlik belched into a fist. "Got any soda?" he asked.

Greene thumbed over his shoulder. "You know where the kitchen is."

"Any idea who did it?" Pavlik asked.

"The generic Vignieri family," Greene said.

"You're a big help, Dex."

"Only for my friends. So what about this opera thing? You really know about this shit?"

"Something about it."

Greene looked at the back of an NYU adult education pamphlet. "Who wrote *Rigoletto?*" he asked.

"Verdi composed it."

"Huh?"

"Verdi."

"*The Barber of Seville.*"

"Rossini."

"*The Elixir of Love.*"

"Donizetti."

"Shit."

Pavlik smiled. "Don't feel bad, Dex. I don't have a fucking clue who wrote *Porgie and Bess.*"

"You're a big one alright," the fat man whispered.

"Huh?" Mangino said, somewhat confused.

"You," the fat man whispered again. He pointed to his left biceps as he curled his arm to show the muscle. "You're big."

"Oh, yeah," Mangino said. "Right."

They were standing in the bathroom of a hotel room watching the filming going on in the king-size bed across the room. A short blond woman was straddled over one man's face while she performed fellatio on a muscular man standing to one side of the bed. The fat man with Mangino was dressed in a black and red sweat suit. Mangino was in black slacks and a tight white turtleneck.

"My wife might like to go a few rounds with you," the fat man said.

"She isn't half bad herself," Mangino said. He was watching the fat man's wife give head to the muscular man on the edge of the bed.

"If you don't mind being filmed, that is," the fat man said. "It's our only requirement."

"I'll have to pass," Mangino said.

They watched the filming for a few minutes longer before Mangino led the fat man into the adjoining room. There the two men poured themselves drinks from a makeshift bar that had been arranged on a small round table.

"So, what did you have in mind?" the fat man asked Mangino.

"A gang bang," Mangino said. "Or a two-on-one, whichever is easier for you to arrange. It has to be private, though. Black and white if you can do it. The girl is white."

"Hmmmm," the fat man said. "Sounds good to me."

"With a very hot broad," Mangino said. "Twenty-seven years hot."

The fat man shifted his eyebrows. "What's the catch?" he asked in a whiny voice.

"She'll be drugged," Mangino said. "Fucked-up drugged. She won't know what's happening."

The fat man held a finger to his lips. "Oh, that's rape," he said nervously. "I don't know that anyone will want to participate in something like that."

"What if they don't know?" Mangino asked. "If you can convince them it's part of the show, the broad being fucked-up."

The fat man looked up at the ceiling. "Hmmmm," he said again. "I'd still have to pay them, whomever we find to do this."

Mangino lit a cigarette. "Absolutely," he said. "And this would be strictly between you and me, of course. For which I'd be willing to return a few favors. Film a movie for free. Give you the space for a movie for free. Whatever you want."

"What are the chances this would come back to haunt us?" the fat man asked.

"No chance," Mangino said. "For either. We'd just be taking the girl where she wants to go. She's a dancer."

"Why does she need to be drugged."

Mangino opened his hands as he shrugged. "Haven't you ever fucked a broad, fooled around with a married broad, she needed to smoke some weed, have a few drinks, to justify what she was about to do for herself? That's what this would be like. She told me she wants to make a move into the business but she needs to be fucked up the first time. The first few times is what she actually said. She wants it to be seduction-like. Like she doesn't want it at first but then does later. You know what I'm saying?"

"What about Eugene?" the fat man asked. "I'm used to dealing with him. I don't want to do an end run on him. He's been very good to us."

Mangino waved the thought off. "Gene's indisposed," he said. He rubbed at the tip of his nose with an index finger. "He let the habit get out of control."

The fat man frowned sympathetically. "That's too bad," he said. "I liked Eugene."

"And he liked you," Mangino said. "But the guys who own the hotel can't have a doper in charge. You know how it goes."

"I didn't think his habit was that bad," the fat man said. "I knew he used. Who doesn't. But I thought he handled himself well."

Mangino opened his hands again. "What can I tell you?"

"Who else would know about this woman?" the fat man asked, changing the subject back to business.

"Me and her boyfriend," Mangino said. "As chaperons. What

more could you want than that?"

The fat man thought about it. "Hmmmm," he said one more time. "I like the images forming in my head."

"Wait'll you see her image," Mangino said.

The fat man bit at his lower lip. "We'll do it here, the filming?" he asked.

"I'd rather not," Mangino said. "I was thinking out by one of the airports someplace. Kennedy or LaGuardia. You know those dumps just off the highway?"

"Sure," the fat man said. "But we'll have to rent more than one room."

Mangino slapped three hundred-dollar bills into the fat man's right hand. "Rent them," he said.

The fat man stashed the money inside his sweatpants back pocket. He looked Mangino up and down one more time. "You're sure about passing on my wife?" he asked.

Mangino winked as he slapped the fat man on the arm. "Maybe some other time," he said.

Chapter 17

The call had come early in the morning. A ten-year-old black boy had been found dead. His body had been strapped over the end of a rotting couch in an abandoned building in Chelsea. The boy had been raped and tortured for days. The murder had been filmed. A VCR tape had been left behind by the killer.

Pavlik was the homicide detective on call the morning the boy's body was found. His partner, Dexter Greene, was on vacation the same week. Pavlik took the call by himself. The crime scene had changed his life forever.

He pursued the investigation in a relentless effort of footwork, research and personal surveillance. A single description of the possible killer provided by a homeless drug addict was all he had to work with.

"He looked like a teacher," the homeless addict had told him. "One of them young yuppie types. A neat boy with blond hair and blue eyes."

Pavlik spent the next twenty-eight consecutive hours examining Board of Education records of a dozen schools in the surrounding vicinity of the crime scene. An upscale private school on the perimeter of the area he researched had hired a substitute teacher who seemed to match the description of the man the homeless addict had given Pavlik. Timothy Waller, a boyish-looking thirty-year-old man with short hair and blue eyes had taught an English class for eighty-five dollars per day.

He managed to find Waller at one of two forwarding addresses the killer had left the school to forward his Board of Education checks. Pavlik followed Waller for the next two days. The FBI had been called in because of the abduction of a wealthy Long Island couple's ten-year-old boy. They had started their investigation by following Pavlik's lead.

Two days later, when Timothy Waller drove out to a secluded area of Far Rockaway in Queens, Pavlik hoped that he wasn't too late.

Inside the abandoned two-family house in Queens, Pavlik found camera equipment stacked near the first floor stairway. When he heard footsteps directly above him, Pavlik drew his gun and climbed the stairs slowly. In the master bedroom of the abandoned house, Timothy Waller had set up a temporary photography studio. He was busy removing a wall backdrop when Pavlik surprised him.

"Where's the kid?" Pavlik had asked Waller.

Waller had turned slowly toward Pavlik and smiled. "You got me," he said. "And it's about time."

"Where's the kid?" Pavlik had repeated.

"He's alive," Waller said. "Smile, detective, you definitely saved his life."

Pavlik had been clenching his teeth. "Where is he?" he asked one more time.

"The basement," Waller had said. "We're finished shooting up here."

In the basement Pavlik found the ten-year-old naked, tied,

and gagged. The boy lay in shock on a single mattress on a roach-infested floor. The boy's eyes were fixed on the wall directly ahead of him. He had been raped and tortured.

Pavlik had already cuffed Waller. When he saw the boy and the condition he was in, Pavlik started to tremble. He forced himself to holster his weapon.

"He's a good boy," Waller had said as Pavlik removed the boy's restraints. "He only cried the first few minutes. He was pretty much mute after the first time. I guess I really didn't have to gag him."

It was then Pavlik completely lost control and started a twenty-two minute bare-fisted assault on Timothy Waller's abdomen. Pavlik caused severe internal bleeding while breaking five of the killer's ribs. The FBI arrived along with the backup Pavlik had called in prior to entering the abandoned house. They stopped Pavlik from punching Timothy Waller to death.

One of Waller's cameras had already been positioned before Pavlik found the killer. Beside the rape and torture of the boy, the camera had also recorded the entire twenty-two minute beating Pavlik had given Waller. The FBI had confiscated the tape.

Pavlik had since relived the scene in his sleep several times. When he woke up from his latest nightmare, he was in a cold sweat. Aelish was sitting up beside him in bed with a cold towel at the ready. She applied it to his forehead as soon as Pavlik sat up.

"You have to talk this out, love," she told him.

"I can't," Pavlik said.

"You have to."

"I can't. I won't. You don't know what it's like. Those kids. The one he killed. I'm not sure which is better off."

"The department provides the service and you should use it," Aelish said.

Pavlik sprang out of the bed and headed into the bathroom. He turned the shower on and let the cold water run a few minutes before he stepped under it.

The Korean man set two packages of cocaine on the back desk in the Manager's office at the Brooklyn Inn hotel. He folded his arms as he waited for Tranchatta to open one of the two bags with a pocketknife.

Tranchatta pointed to a large white envelope on the couch. "Take a look at those, you need something to do," he said.

He had just returned from the emergency room at Coney Island Hospital. His right forearm and hand were bandaged where he had been burned the day before. He held the package in place by leaning on it with his right elbow.

The Korean man opened the white envelope and smiled. The envelope contained a thick stack of pornographic photographs. The Korean man removed the pictures and went through them one by one.

"You don't ret me in on porn business, why?" the Korean man asked with a heavy accent. "I find prenty of customer."

"Define prenty," Tranchatta said. He rubbed resin from the cocaine on his teeth.

"White man rove Asian girr porn," the Korean man said. "Same with Korean man and white girr. Asian girr with brack man, Asian girr with white man, Asian girr with animah, make no difference. Asian girr make market bigger."

"You got a point," Tranchatta said.

The Korean man was nodding enthusiastically. "Good business," he said. "Expand market. Asian girr expand market." He examined a picture of a black woman with two white men. "I rike this," he said. "Brack woman with white man. I rike this."

"I'll get you a copy of the tape before you leave," Tranchatta said. "What's the name on the back of the picture?"

The Korean man flipped the picture and read the name printed in red ink aloud: "Doris. You know Doris?"

"If you're a good boy I'll get you a date with Doris," Tranchatta said. "Half-hour date in one of the rooms upstairs."

The Korean man smiled. "I rike Doris," he said. He slipped the picture inside his front pants pocket. "I bring you Asian girr," he said. "Good brow job girr. Take big one, rike this, orr way down."

Tranchatta looked up and saw the Korean man holding his hands about a foot apart. "That's great," Tranchatta said, without emotion.

"Big brack man, big white man, big Asian man," the Korean man continued. "Take hoe thing, orr way down. You make movie. Asian girr movie. Asian girr with big brack man."

"I have enough blow job movies," Tranchatta said. "I have too many blow job movies."

"What happened your hand?" the Korean man asked.

Tranchatta glanced down at his bandaged hand. "Some psycho burned it," he said.

The Korean man continued flipping through the still shots. "Girrfriend? You don't make her happy, she burn you?" He held up one picture. "This her, you girrfriend?"

"Very funny," Tranchatta said. "Don't mix those up, alright."

The Korean man licked at the picture he was holding. It was a tiny woman with a big man. He held it up. "This girr very pretty," he said. He turned the picture over to find a name. "Jenny?" he asked.

"Yeah, yeah," Tranchatta said. "When's the next delivery? I might have to change the location."

The Korean man shrugged. "Two weeks. I don't know."

Tranchatta counted twenty stacks of one-hundred dollar bills on the desk. "Here, take this before somebody else does," he said.

The Korean man slipped the picture of the small woman inside his front pants pocket. "Maybe you need Korean girrfriend," he said. "I have girr make you very happy. Two girr. Sister. I bring next time. You make movie. Asian movie. Two girr. Sister."

Tranchatta bagged up the product and wiped his desk clean while the Korean man stashed the money inside a small gym bag.

"What you say, I bring you two sister?" the Korean man continued.

"Yeah, well, don't bother," he said. "I got enough girlfriends, I want them." He looked at his watch and wiped sweat from his forehead.

"Why you no want partner?" the Korean man asked. "Korean girr make you very happy. Suck your dick orr day, you want."

Tranchatta stashed the product inside the second drawer of his desk and locked it.

"We make deah," the Korean man said. He was holding up another picture of the small woman. "You give me her, one hour, I give you Korean sister girr, one hour. Two for one."

Tranchatta smirked as he motioned at the Korean with his head. "You're just a dirty old bastard, huh?" he said.

The Korean man smiled again. "Maybe you rike Korean girr. Make movie with them. They take big dick orr the way." He was holding his hands apart again. "Big brack man, rike this."

"That be a waste of energy, pal," Tranchatta said. "I'm not that big."

"I bring them anyway. Maybe you make movie, okay? You no have Asian girr here." He held up the white envelope. "Asian girr add customer."

Tranchatta seemed to be thinking about it. "What else can you do for me?" he asked. "Besides the blow job I don't need."

"What you want?" the Korean man asked. "Anything for friend. Anything for partner. You terr me what you need."

Tranchatta looked at his bandaged hand. "I'll let you know," he said.

Chapter 18

Pavlik knocked on the passenger window of the Ford Taurus and DeNafria unlocked the doors from the inside. Pavlik sat in the front seat and handed DeNafria a cup of coffee.

"I got you milk and sugar," Pavlik said.

"Thanks," DeNafria said.

Pavlik sipped his own coffee. "I had a nightmare," he said. "I get them from time to time. Ever since I busted Waller."

DeNafria was focused on a couple talking in the curb outside his wife's house. The woman, short and lean with her dark hair tied up, was DeNafria's wife, Jody. She was talking to a tall lean man with blond hair and a muscular build. The man appeared a few years younger than the woman.

"Huh?" DeNafria said.

"I had a nightmare about busting Waller again," Pavlik said.

"Oh," DeNafria said. "You talk to the department counselor?"

"No," Pavlik said. "I can't bring myself to talk to strangers about it. But I still dream about that piece of shit and what he did to those kids. And then a guy like this Mangino comes along and somehow I group him together with Waller."

DeNafria was back to studying his wife and the man she was with. "Huh?" he said.

"You're preoccupied," Pavlik said. "What's up?"

"That's my wife," DeNafria said. "I don't know the guy."

"Across the street?"

"Yeah."

"Uh-oh."

"I think she was trying to send me a message with my kid earlier in the week," DeNafria said. "She had him ask me if I was dating. I took it the wrong way. I guess she meant she was about to."

"How long you been here?"

"Since I beeped you. Half hour or so."

Pavlik sipped his coffee again. "This isn't good," he said.

"I know," DeNafria said. "I didn't expect to find this."

"What did you expect?" Pavlik asked.

"She didn't say anything," DeNafria said. "She didn't tell me, you know. I expected she'd tell me about something like this."

"Look, John, I'm not so sure this is a good idea," Pavlik said. "I think you should back off."

"We're separated less than a year," DeNafria said. "Ten months, to be exact. This is wrong, man. It's wrong."

Pavlik let a few moments pass. He saw that DeNafria was still focused on the situation across the street.

"I appreciate you're telling me first but I'm still a little uncomfortable," Pavlik said. "We shouldn't be here."

"You can take off if you want," DeNafria said without looking at Pavlik.

"I don't want to take off," Pavlik said. "Not on you. I'm just not comfortable doing this. It's awkward."

"How do you think I feel," DeNafria said. "I didn't know this would happen. I didn't expect this. I was coming by to drop off the damn Jets tickets. So the kid could hold them in his hands."

"Or maybe it was an excuse to drop in on your wife," Pavlik said.

DeNafria glared at Pavlik.

"I'm just saying," Pavlik said. "Suggesting. Maybe there's more to it. Maybe you should back off."

DeNafria shifted the Taurus into gear and burned rubber on the street. He sped directly pass his wife and the man she was with. He was sure she had turned her head and had seen him.

"I was coming to give the kid the tickets," DeNafria said after he had turned onto an avenue.

"Right," Pavlik said. "And that little show burning rubber was to test the Michelins."

They drove the rest of the way into Manhattan in silence. The few times Pavlik tried to start a conversation, DeNafria shook his head to end it.

Finally, when they parked outside the Corinthian Condominiums luxury apartment building where Larry Berra lived, DeNafria apologized.

"I didn't mean to drag you into that," he said. "I'm sorry."

"Forget it," Pavlik said. "I'm just looking out for you. I went through that once myself. Only I wasn't blessed with a kid. Be grateful, no matter what happens between you and your wife. You have your son."

DeNafria nodded.

The concierge told the two detectives that Larry Berra had left earlier and hadn't returned yet. DeNafria left his card with the concierge and told him to make sure Mr. Berra knew the police had come.

Outside the luxury apartment building, DeNafria pulled a cigarette from a fresh pack. Pavlik lit it for him.

"Thanks," DeNafria said.

"You think this guy is for real?" Pavlik asked.

"Berra wanting to talk to us?" Questioned DeNafria.

Pavlik fingered a cigarette from his own pack.

"I think he's probably scared," DeNafria said. "I think he's nervous about what Mangino did to Lucia. Maybe. Maybe he finally realizes it's not a game anymore, his attempt at being a gangster."

Pavlik lit his cigarette. "But there's no way Lucia will talk, huh?"

"Not in this lifetime."

Pavlik took a long drag on the cigarette. "You think they'll try her again?"

"I doubt it."

Both men were quiet while they smoked. Then DeNafria asked, "What do you mean, you went through it once yourself?"

Pavlik let out a long stream of smoke. "My first wife," he said. "We were married just under three years. She met somebody right before I went undercover. I got a promotion and she got a lover. She broke it to me the same night I got the promotion. 'We have to talk,' she said. You get that?"

DeNafria nodded. "More or less. What you do?"

"At first? Promised myself I'd kill the guy. I'd find him and shoot him and then shoot myself."

"And when you didn't do that?"

Pavlik stretched his long arms behind him as he yawned. "I

asked my father to look into it for me," he said. "He was a cop, too. He retired a detective. He found out she had another boyfriend before the one she told me about. At least that's what he told me. It convinced me to not ruin my life over it. I moved out while they were at a hotel. I had my lawyer call her. I served her papers and that was it."

DeNafria made a face. "That was it?"

"I drank," Pavlik said. "Like a fish. But not enough to turn alcoholic. Close but no cigar. Then I found out she got dumped by the boyfriend, after he made her pregnant. Somehow that made me feel better. We were both too young. It never would have lasted anyway. I stopped drinking after that."

"It's killing me," DeNafria said. "But that drink sounds good. Maybe I'll give it a shot."

"It's no solution but it will numb the pain," Pavlik said. "Of course there's always work. Nailing this punk Mangino might serve you just as good as a bottle."

DeNafria furrowed his eyebrows. "You really have it for him, huh?"

Pavlik tightened his lips. "Yep," he said. "I really do."

It was cool and breezy in the Luna Park projects in Coney Island. Benny Luchessi and Jimmy Mangino sat on the top of a bench back and watched the softball game being played on the asphalt softball field. Luchessi was smoking a cigarette. Mangino chewed on a pretzel with mustard.

"The thing of it is," Luchessi was saying, "Joe Sharpetti made his first million in porn. It's not like the guy is a saint, it comes to that stuff."

"Porn don't make him a bad person," Mangino said. "It's where the money has always been."

The softball pinged off an aluminum bat as a tall thin kid lined a single to left field.

"No, it doesn't," Luchessi said. "But now the guy is supervising the cleanup of the stuff and he's taking it a little too fucking serious, you ask me."

"Jack Fama says Joe Sharp just likes to hear himself talk is all," Mangino said. He licked mustard off his finger.

"Except when he orders a hit," Luchessi said. "Three of them not too long ago."

"The Canarsie pier thing," Mangino said.

"On orders, yeah, but from what I understand, when the skippers got together to discuss it, nobody heard Joe Sharp complaining about taking out three guys made this family a lot of money over the years."

"Which is one reason Jack Fama isn't so loyal to his skipper anymore," Mangino said.

"'Jackie Slick' is loyal to his cock," Luchessi said. "Nobody says nothing because he's a Vignieri by blood. We like having him with us on this but don't let your personal feelings get in the way, Jimmy. This turns into the war it could turn into, between Sharpetti's crew and our crew, don't be surprised Jack Fama is measuring the wind at every turn, he don't put one in your back. Fama is a pretty boy Sicilian who wants the same thing as everybody else anxious enough to get involved in our thing. He wants to be boss someday."

Mangino watched a heavy man hit a fast pitch over the center field fence. The F-train was passing on the trestle above the fence. The ball struck the F-train on one of the front wheels.

"Mingatta," Mangino said. "That was some shot."

"I'm meeting Larry later today," Luchessi said. "His asshole is bleeding about something."

"I think it's good, he's nervous," Mangino said.

"Just don't fuck it up," Luchessi said. "This kid is like a walking lotto ticket. Whatever you're planning on, make sure it involves squeezing him."

"Like a grapefruit," Mangino said.

Luchessi lit a fresh cigarette. "And Eugene?" he asked.

"Jack Fama is coming along," Mangino said. "Just to solidify things."

"He say that, he'll be there?"

"He'll try, he said," Mangino said. "Maybe he can't. Depends on the time."

Luchessi laughed. "Don't be surprised he don't show."

"Jack? Why not?"

"Because of what you just said," Luchessi said. "It solidifies things if he's with you on this. He'll want to leave himself an out. A guy like him will always leave himself an out."

Mangino lit his own cigarette. "Well, he put me up in a hideaway apartment and he said he'll try to be there with this thing."

"Just don't count on it," Luchessi said. "And remember it has to get done."

"I'll take care of it," Mangino said. "Either way. With or without him. I'll take care of it."

Luchessi slapped Mangino on the leg. "Which is why you're getting straightened out," he said.

Mangino leaned back at the surprise. "Really? Serious? I'm getting made?"

Luchessi nodded.

"Great," Mangino said. "Not that I don't deserve it. It is about time and all."

Luchessi nudged Mangino with an elbow. "Easy, Maverick," he said.

"Thanks," Mangino said. "It's nice to hear it."

"You earned it."

Mangino was feeling proud. He sat up straight. "Can I ask when?"

"Nobody ever knows when," Luchessi said. "You'll get a call and you'll have enough time to get dressed. They'll pick you up and that will be that."

Mangino clapped for himself. "Nice," he said. "This makes my day."

Luchessi nudged Mangino with an elbow again. "It was supposed to," he said.

Chapter 19

In the manager's office of the Brooklyn Inn, Eugene Tranchatta glanced at a stack of porn still shots of two Korean girls with several different men. He set the pictures down on the desk and lit a cigarette. The two Asian men who had brought the pictures stood side-by-side in the office. They were tall and skinny. They looked to be somewhere in their twenties. Tranchatta pointed to the couch. The Asian men sat.

"I told your boss I needed something else," he told them. "I need protection."

The Asian men were both dressed in black satin shirts and black slacks. The taller of the two spoke in broken English. "We are protection. We take care of problem."

Tranchatta looked the two men over and let out a deep breath. "This guy would eat you two for breakfast," he said. "I hope you brought something with you."

"Not worry," the Asian man said. "We brought something."

"Good," Tranchatta said. "And feel free to use it, whatever you brought. This guy is a genuine prick but he's a tough prick."

"We take care," the Asian said.

"Yeah, you said. What time you guys coming back?"

"After twelve, midnight."

"Just make sure you show. I got a bad feeling about tonight."

"No worry. We be here."

"Right," Tranchatta said. "I'd like a half-a-buck for every fuckin no worry I heard in my life didn't come back to bite me on the balls. I'd like a dime, I'd still do alright."

The Asian was confused. "No understand," he said.

"Nor will you ever," Tranchatta said. He took a quick nervous drag on his cigarette. "Just be here after midnight. And try to catch him outside. He's got a red Trans Am. He parks out back."

Both of the Asian men stood up. "We be here later," the taller one said. He turned and guided his friend out of the office.

Tranchatta watched the two men leave the office. He was lighting a fresh cigarette when the telephone rang. He jumped from the sound and dropped the cigarette onto the floor. He started to pick the cigarette up and stepped on it by accident instead.

"Great," he said aloud. "Nothing is going right."

Jack Fama met his contact with the Federal Bureau of Investigation in a synagogue on Avenue U in Brooklyn. The temple was quiet. Both men stood in a dark hallway under a dim light.

"I'm supposed to give this barber some shit later today," Jack Fama told Special Agent John Feller.

Feller was a heavyset middle-aged man with a thick neck and broad shoulders. He had thick eyebrows and piercing eyes. He tried to look into Fama's eyes whenever the mobster spoke.

"Yeah, and what else?" Feller asked. He had a deep husky voice.

"First I'm supposed to help Mangino whack some guy, Eugene Tranchatta," Fama continued. "But I already got out of that because of Joe Sharp's bullshit meetings on the boardwalk."

"He fell for that?" Feller asked. "Joe Sharp doesn't even acknowledge your existence."

"What the hell does Jimmy Mangino know?" Fama said. "He is away for two years. Just come out."

"Who's he whacking?"

"I said, but you don't listen," Fama said. "Eugene Tranchatta. Some guy from the hotel in Brooklyn. Something about drugs. He wants to intercept a drug deal, take the money and drugs."

"For Luchessi?"

Fama glanced at his watch. "I have to be in Coney Island soon," he said.

"For what?" Feller asked. "You enter the hot dog contest at Nathans?"

Fama forced a sarcastic smile. "I don't talk to Joe Sharp but I have to report in," he said.

"And what about the barber?" Feller asked.

"He want me to terrorize him," Fama said. "Go to the house in Sheepshead Bay and give him and his wife some shit. He wants to try and collect some of the money the guy owes somebody else. I don't know who he owes. He told me to scare the old man. To shake him up."

"When do you meet Luchessi?" Feller asked.

"Maybe I don't," Fama said. "Nobody tell me."

Feller was annoyed at another vague answer. "We're not interested in Jimmy Mangino. We need Luchessi."

"Luchessi is with another crew," Fama said as he pointed at himself. "What you want from me?"

"It's what you want from us, Jack," Feller reminded Fama. "To stay in America and play the slick bad guy. Instead of going back to Sicily and spending the rest of your life getting fucked in the ass by all those guys already inside the prisons there who know you fucked their wives."

"You fucking guys," Fama said. "All the time breaking balls, eh? All the time make remark."

"I can't help it I don't like you, Jack," Feller said. "You make it hard to like you."

Fama glanced at his watch again. "I have to go soon," he said. "Coney Island is fifteen minute from here."

"It's more like ten," Feller said. "Just make sure you don't get carried away with the old man, okay? Shake up but don't break up, *capisce?*"

"Io capisco," Fama said.

Feller pointed toward the end of the hallway and smiled. *"Ciao,"* he said.

Chapter 20

"He's with this guy?" Pavlik said. He handed DeNafria a department mug shot of Benjamin Luchessi.

DeNafria immediately recognized the gangster. He set the white paper bag with the coffees on the console of the Ford Taurus. "Larry's nervous about something," DeNafria said. "This is the wiseguy normally bleeds Larry. The guy he normally runs crying to."

They were parked on Lafayette Street in SoHo. The trendy restaurant off the corner of Bleeker Street was busy. A small line of patrons waited in a line outside the restaurant.

"They went in together half-an-hour ago," Pavlik said. He removed one of the coffee containers from the paper bag.

"The girl there?" DeNafria asked. "Larry's arm piece, Leanna."

"Nope, but she was," Pavlik said. "For about two minutes. And guess who she arrived with? Who drove her."

DeNafria removed the other container from the bag.

"Mangino," Pavlik said without waiting for an answer.

DeNafria's head snapped back. "You sure?"

"Positive. He dropped her off twenty yards from the restaurant, then pulled further up the block to wait for her. She went in and came out and got right back in his Trans Am. Unless it was stolen. They turned west on Houston."

"Larry's piece of tail and Jimmy Bench-Press," DeNafria said. "Don't that make for interesting conversation."

Pavlik sipped his coffee. "So why is he with this guy, Luchessi?" he asked. "He doesn't want our help anymore?"

DeNafria removed the cap from the coffee container. "Who knows," he said. "But the girl and Mangino are what I'm wondering about. Does Larry know about them is the question of the day?"

"I doubt it," Pavlik said.

"Me, too," DeNafria said.

Pavlik sipped some more coffee. "What did he say to you, this jerkoff inside?"

DeNafria was stirring his coffee with a plastic stick. "Maybe he thinks Mangino wants to kill him," he said. "He didn't bother to tell the barber much except he needed to talk to us. Maybe Larry does know about the girl."

"Maybe the girl and Mangino are out to whack Larry," Pavlik said.

DeNafria sipped his coffee as he glanced at his watch. "Why whack him if the guy is worth more alive than dead?"

"My point being, maybe we should sit on Mangino and the girl," Pavlik said. "Just in case. It worked for me once before, following a guy I had a suspicion about."

"Well, I'd forget the girl. She won't be involved in that. Not to the point she'd be there. Besides, I don't see Benny Luchessi letting go of a gravy train like Larry Berra."

"What if he does kill somebody?" Pavlik asked. "This isn't going to turn into another round of let's make a deal, I hope. I been through that once already and it isn't pretty."

"Mangino?" DeNafria asked.

"Yeah, Mangino," Pavlik said.

"He kills someone, we get him for murder," DeNafria said. "But I wouldn't dream too hard about that. That would be an O.C. wet dream, to do surveillance on a guy you're trying to turn and he whacks somebody."

Pavlik let out a breath of frustration. "I guess I don't get it," he said.

"It's the nature of the beast," DeNafria said. "We'd like to flip Larry Berra, if we could get Benny Luchessi, say, but we'll take whomever we can get. Jimmy Bench-Press has been around long enough to offer up somebody in a deal of his own, too, now."

Pavlik made a face.

"Hey, you never know," DeNafria said. "He hasn't flipped in the past because he wasn't looking at enough time. Hopefully the guy Jimmy gives up is connected enough to offer up somebody else. This flipping thing works because of the network these guys establish. The more contacts they make, the better our chances. We'd like Berra but we'll take Mangino. Besides, if Mangino flips on Berra, on whatever deal they made together, Berra will definitely flip on whomever he's dealing with, Benjamin Luchessi for one. Benny's a made guy. Who knows who he'll flip on."

"And whomever dies along the way is what? What do you call them?" Pavlik asked.

"Unlucky," DeNafria said. "Not to sound cold, but that's what they are, unlucky. They're involved in a game where getting killed is one of the consequences. That's not our fault."

Pavlik remained silent.

"Is this a homicide thing?" DeNafria asked.

"What's that?"

"What you seem to be going through," DeNafria said. "Because if you're looking for the justice angle in this area, organized crime, you're not going to find it very often. This is scumbag central, O.C."

"It would be nice, to know something might happen to that prick," Pavlik said.

"Mangino?"

"Yeah, Mangino."

"This about the other day?"

"It's about everything. What he did to get inside a jail the first two times and what he's done since he's out. He deserves a beating, yeah. He doesn't deserve to be out playing the bully, terrorizing an old man, beating up a woman. It's about all the bullshit we're supposed to be stopping."

DeNafria held up his hands. "Look, I can't make you any guarantees about what may or may not happen to Jimmy Mangino," he said. "But I can guarantee you this, if you're stuck on that issue, the justice angle, organized crime isn't the place for you."

"I didn't ask for organized crime," Pavlik said.

"I know," DeNafria said. "Neither of us did."

At a table in the back of the Italian restaurant, Bella Rosa, Larry Berra sat with Benjamin Luchessi in a booth eating lunch. The two men were eating salads and drinking white wine. Luchessi wore a black nylon sweat suit. Berra was dressed in a gray suit with a pink shirt and red tie. He wiped at his mouth with a cloth napkin.

"He got my girl's head turned around," Berra said. "And he did a job for me where he might've gone overboard."

Luchessi sipped his wine. "What do you mean got her head turned around?" he asked.

Berra leaned in close and whispered. "He's banging her," he said.

Luchessi coughed from choking. He needed a sip of water before he could compose himself. "I take it you love this broad," he said.

"Very much," Berra said.

"Then he did you a favor," Luchessi said through some more coughing. "When your head clears, you think about it again. He did you a big favor."

"But it was disrespectful," Berra said. "He knew who she was to me."

Luchessi waved a finger at Berra. "You're not a made guy," he said. "He fucked a loose broad is what he did. The fact he told you, he did you a favor. If it's a matter of class, that he don't have any, that's another story. That don't make him a bad person."

Berra was nervous. He wiped sweat from his forehead. "He's got a game plan to take me," he said. "Leanna told me Mangino is making plans to take me for a lot of money."

"Leanna, please," Luchessi said. He waved the name off. "She's the one with her pants down, no? Please."

"He's out of control," Berra said.

"Except he went and did what you paid him to do," Luchessi said. "Right or no? He told you he'd do something and he did it. Now he's telling you he has something else he can do. Why don't you wait and see maybe the guy gets you some of that money you gave away. You come to me for this bullshit but you didn't bother to ask me about giving sixty grand to a fucking barber. Your father'd be turning in his grave."

"What if Leanna is telling the truth?" Berra asked.

"Then I'll take care of him," Luchessi said. "Until then, until you got proof other than some twat screwing half the city behind your back, it looks like you got somebody can protect some of the investments you got no business in. I'd let it ride a little longer before I panicked about Jimmy Mangino. The guy's hungry is all. He's been away. He wasn't the one with everything to lose. Your girlfriend, Leanna, whatever her name is, is the one with something to lose. Not for nothin', kid, the way she walks around, your girl. Like today, for instance, her clothes all skimpy and tight like that? Don't get me wrong, she's a looker, but she wants to be looked at. The way she was today, I mean. Me, if she's my broad? I wouldn't allow it." He shook his head. "I just wouldn't allow it."

Berra sat in obedient silence.

Luchessi wiped his mouth with a napkin again. "Now," he said. "You got my envelope or you need to go get it."

Berra slipped a thick envelope from his right front pants pocket and handed it to Luchessi under the table.

"There you go," Luchessi said.

Berra forced a smile.

Luchessi patted Berra on the forearm. "Don't worry about it," he said. "Everything will work out. You'll dump this broad likes to fuck around, you'll get some of your money back from that fiasco with the barber, and you got Uncle Benny looking out for you. Your father was a good man, I owe him at least that much."

Berra swallowed hard at the mention of his father.

Luchessi nibbled at a piece of Italian bread. "You'll do fine by this guy, Jimmy Mangino," he told Berra. "He needs to learn some manners but he gets the job done. Like I said, he did you two favors already."

Berra lost his smile.

Luchessi slapped Berra on the arm again. "You're a good boy," he said. "You'll make out fine in the end."

Chapter 21

It was just after two o'clock in the morning. Tranchatta and the Russian man sat in the Brooklyn Inn lounge sipping vodka from shot glasses. They had completed their drug deal a few hours earlier. The Russian man was tired. His eyes were red.

"Where is this focking guy?" he said with an accent. He glanced at his watch. "I tell him one o'clock to pick me up."

Tranchatta handed the Russian man half a dozen still photographs of two Korean sisters. The Russian man sniffled, as he looked the pictures over.

"There are more," Tranchatta said. "But I don't want to waste my time or theirs, or yours for that matter, if you already made up your mind. These cunts are looking to finance a movie and you can have the inside track."

The Russian man looked at the pictures again, then at his watch. "Let me see rest," he said.

Tranchatta frowned. "You sure?"

The Russian man refilled his shot glass with vodka from the open bottle on the bar. "Let me see, let me see," he said.

Tranchatta pulled out another envelope of still shots. The two Asian women were grouped with up to five men in a dozen different pictures. The Russian showed no expression as he examined them.

"Good," he finally said. "Bring them next week."

"I have to arrange that," Tranchatta said. "With our Korean friend. This was all he gave me. He sent a couple guys with them earlier. What about a fee?"

"What about it?" the Russian asked back.

"I do for you, you do for me," Tranchatta said.

The Russian downed another shot of vodka. "What you want?"

"For you to take care of a problem I have," he said.

"What problem?"

"A guy."

"What guy? Stop playing games."

"A guy leaning on me. A big guy."

"Italian wiseguy?"

"No, nothing like that," Tranchatta said. "Although he probably has friends somewhere."

"What you want, Eugene?"

"I want him backed off," Tranchatta said. "He thinks he's my partner because of something else. He's starting to push his weight around here. He did this to my arm." He picked up the sleeve of his shirt and showed the Russian his bandage. "He burned me."

The Russian rubbed his eyes. "How am I back off, Eugene?" he asked.

"You got friends, Vladi," Tranchatta said. "I know you do."

"You mean Russian mob," the Russian said. "I have friends, yes. But not to shoot people."

Tranchatta looked around himself. "Who said you should shoot him?"

"How am I to back off then?" the Russian asked. "I'm waiter. I'm making money to bet with. Focking Knicks. Focking Yankees. Mets. Focking Giants and Jets. Hockey. Horses. Card games. Focking 'Lantic City. Focking Blackjack."

"And you finance this movie you make more money to bet with," Tranchatta said. "And you do something for me, with this guy, and I don't have to worry about losing our arrangement. You see what I'm saying."

"I don't focking shoot people," the Russian said.

"You don't have to fucking shoot anybody," Tranchatta said through clenched teeth.

"Focking Reggie Miller kill me last night," the Russian said. "Forty-one point he make."

Tranchatta took a deep breath. "Why don't you go home and sleep it off," he said. "Give it some thought tomorrow and we'll talk then, alright?"

The Russian reached for the vodka bottle one more time but Tranchatta moved it away from him.

"That's enough," Tranchatta said. "I got a couple guys I need to talk to. I'll put you in a cab back to Canarsie."

The Russian man yawned at Tranchatta. "Focking Canarsie," he said.

Two hours later, two Asian men leaned on the back of a sports car a few lanes from where Jimmy Mangino parked his Trans Am. Each of the Asian men was holding a two-foot pipe. They waited for Mangino to step out of his Trans Am before converging toward him.

Mangino stopped in his tracks. He was still carrying the .9mm

Beretta inside the waist of his pants. He opened the jacket he was wearing and touched the handle of the gun.

"What you got there, Jimmy?" one of the Asian men said. "You going to pull out your dick?"

"I know you?" Mangino asked.

The two Asian men were about ten feet from Mangino. They both stopped.

"You like to push people around," the Asian man who had spoke before said. "You like to burn people."

Mangino smiled. "Ah, so Eugene sent you," he said.

"Who's Eugene?" the Asian man asked.

"The bald asshole with the big ears," Mangino said. "The one you bring your drugs to sell."

Both Asian men looked at each other. "You fucking talking about, Jimmy?" the one who did the talking said.

"You two going to kill me?" Mangino asked.

"Maybe."

"Maybe? That's what those pipes are? Maybe?"

"You leave Eugene alone, Jimmy. From now on. You no more partner."

"Really?"

"Or we fucking kill you, man."

Mangino pulled the Beretta from his pants. The two Asian men stepped back.

"Maybe?" Mangino said.

Both men dropped the pipes.

"Now that was stupid," Mangino said. He shot each man in the chest several times before getting back into his car and driving out of the parking lot.

* * *

Eugene Tranchatta took the call from the hotel a few minutes after doing a line of cocaine. It was the bartender at the Brooklyn Inn lounge. He told Tranchatta about the shooting in the hotel parking lot.

Tranchatta's nose was bleeding from the cocaine he had snorted all night. His eyes were bloodshot.

"What do you mean a shooting?" he asked the bartender.

"In the parking lot," the bartender said. "Two guys. Noodles, I think. That's what the cops said. Asians. They were both killed."

"Holy shit," Tranchatta said.

"Yeah," the bartender said. "There's a couple news trucks out back already. The place is swarming with cops. They're all over the hotel. I sent the girls working the lounge home."

"Good," Tranchatta said. "Anybody see Jimmy Bench-Press around tonight?"

"Mangino? Nah, not me. Nobody mentioned him."

"You sure?"

"Yeah, I'm sure. Why, what's up?"

Tranchatta was squinting trying to think. "Nothing," he said. "Just keep it low. Don't give them nothing."

"They're gonna be calling you soon enough," the bartender asked. "They're already asking who runs the place. You might as well come down now."

"I'm all fucked-up," Tranchatta said. "I can't now."

"Then you better not answer your phone," the bartender said. "Or your door."

"Right," Tranchatta said. "I won't."

"All right, then," the bartender said. "Talk to you later."

"Right," Tranchatta said. "I gotta go."

He hung up the phone and wiped sweat from his forehead. He poured himself a tall glass of vodka and filled it with ice cubes. He sat quiet in his living room for several minutes before the doorbell rang. He shut his eyes tight as he sat on his couch in silence. He heard the doorbell ring again but didn't flinch.

He kept his eyes shut tight for what seemed like forever. When he was sure whomever was at the door had gone, he opened his eyes slowly. He remained still until the door was suddenly kicked open.

Tranchatta started to beg for mercy from a fetal position when Jimmy Mangino shot him in the face.

Chapter 22

Pavlik set a bottle of Jack Daniel's Sour Mash next to a bottle of Chivas Regal Scotch on the small coffee table in DeNafria's living room. DeNafria was sitting in his recliner with a towel wrapped around his neck. He had just finished his fifth set of fifty sit-ups. His head was dripping sweat.

"This is a starter set," Pavlik said. "The Jack Daniel's is for you. You got any Coke?"

DeNafria thumbed over his right shoulder. "In the fridge," he said.

Pavlik made his way into the tiny kitchen. He opened the door to the fridge and made a face. Several opened cartons of Chinese food lay on the top shelf. Rows of Fruity juice box drinks took up most of the second shelf. The Coca-Cola cans were scattered on the third shelf among half-wrapped sandwiches that looked stale.

"You think anymore about what Larry Berra's girlfriend is doing with Jimmy Bench-Press?" DeNafria yelled to Pavlik.

"Not a single minute, did I give it any thought," Pavlik said. He was collecting glasses and cans of Coca-Cola for the trip back to the living room. "And I wished to hell you'd stop calling him Jimmy Bench-Press," he said. "It makes him sound much tougher than I'm sure he is."

DeNafria pointed at Pavlik when he was back inside the living room. "You don't like that he's a tough guy, do you?"

Pavlik set the glasses and cans of soda on the coffee table. He opened the Jack Daniel's bottle and poured the sour mash into a highball glass. He filled a quarter of the glass with the liquor.

"I don't like anything about that punk," Pavlik said. "And, yeah, I'd like a crack at him. If that's your next question. I think I can bust him up."

"The guy bench-presses four hundred pounds," DeNafria said. He took the glass from Pavlik and poured his own Coca-Cola on top of the sour mash. "It's a fact, not fiction," DeNafria went on. "It's how he got the name. One wiseguy bet another wiseguy who's meat was stronger. Mangino bench-pressed four hundred and five pounds. That's before he ever went away. Five-six years ago. He might even be stronger now."

"Big fucking deal," Pavlik said. He poured a shot of Chivas Regal into his own highball glass and downed it. He sat on the couch and immediately poured a double shot of the scotch into the glass. He sipped from a can of soda before downing the second shot.

"There," Pavlik said. "Woooooo!"

DeNafria took a stiff drink of the sour mash and soda mix. "This isn't bad," he said.

"It'll kick your ass by the third glass," Pavlik said. "Second glass, you're not used to drinking. But you're a rookie so you need an ass-kicking."

DeNafria took another drink. He set the glass down and leaned back in the recliner. "Mangino really is a tough guy," he told Pavlik. "The guy is big and strong and he can kick ass. It isn't something to be uptight about. I know you were a boxer and all but you don't have to be able to kick everyone's ass."

Pavlik lit a cigarette. "Just the bad guys," he said. "That's when it's important to me. Just the bad guys."

DeNafria sipped at his drink.

Pavlik noticed the computer across the room and pointed to it. "You ever use that thing?" he asked.

"My kid more than me," DeNafria said. "I got it for him."

Pavlik smiled. "A kid," he said.

DeNafria pointed to a row of pictures on the top of the television. "That's Vincent there," he said.

Pavlik sat up straight and squinted to see the pictures. "He's a good-looking kid," he said. "Must look like his mother."

DeNafria stood up and made his way into his bedroom. He brought back a large blue picture album. He opened it to the first picture. DeNafria's wife, Jody, the year they were married, stood in a red bikini on a beach in Puerto Rico.

"His mother is beautiful," DeNafria said.

"Yes she is," Pavlik said. He flipped through the pictures of Jody DeNafria and was soon looking at wedding pictures. He closed the book and set it to one side.

DeNafria was about to sit down again. He stopped when he saw Pavlik had closed the album. "What's wrong?" he asked.

"This is about drinking," Pavlik said. "Two manly men of the law sitting down to tie one on. Trust me, you need it. You need it more than those pictures right now." He held up his drink for a toast. "To manly men of the law!" Pavlik yelled.

DeNafria held up his drink. Pavlik nodded and they drank.

DeNafria finished his first drink. He handed his glass to Pavlik for another. "Ever think about one, a kid? Having one, I mean?" he asked.

Pavlik waved his free hand. "No," he said. "Not until I grow up myself. I'm not ready."

"That didn't stop me," DeNafria said.

Pavlik poured DeNafria's drink and held out the glass. "Exactly," he said.

After an hour or so, both men were feeling the booze they had consumed. Both the sour mash and scotch bottles were one quarter gone. Pavlik lay slumped on the couch. An ashtray lay on his stomach with a cigarette burning away in it. DeNafria had reclined in his chair. He was staring up at the ceiling. He chewed on a plastic swizzle stick. He glanced over at Pavlik.

"I wanted to be a baseball player when I was growing up," DeNafria said.

"I wanted to be a war hero when I was ten," Pavlik said. He reached for his cigarette and saw a long gray ash was hanging. He flicked the ash off and took a quick last drag on what was left.

"You play war when you were a kid?" DeNafria asked.

Pavlik lit a fresh cigarette. "New man," he said. "That's what we used to say after we got shot. New man. I was always Sergeant Saunders from *Combat*. You watch that?"

"When we were kids, who didn't?" DeNafria said.

"Then I kept changing my mind," Pavlik said. "I wanted to be a wrestler. I hate to admit it now but I used to root for a guinea back then. Bruno Sammartino. I got his autograph once outside the automat when I was a kid. I thought he was God. My father couldn't stand that I liked Bruno but there were no good guy Polish champs back then."

"Bruno was a god in my house, too," DeNafria said. "Especially with my grandfather. Bruno used to do those impassioned speeches after he was jumped during an interview, remember? Somebody would hit him on the back with a folding chair or something. They'd rip up the suit he was wearing and my grandfather would sit on the edge of the armchair in the living room and get all excited when Bruno spoke Italian."

Pavlik was laughing. "Then I wanted to be a rock-and-roll drummer," he said. "I loved Ginger Baker and Cream. Jack Bruce and Eric Clapton."

"You got me there," DeNafria said. "I wasn't allowed to listen to rock. It was Frank Sinatra, Dean Martin, Mario Lanza and when Pavarotti came along, that was it. Just Pavarotti."

"You into opera?" Pavlik asked.

DeNafria shrugged. "I can take it or leave it," he said. "Some of the arias are nice enough. I prefer Sinatra."

Pavlik took a long drag on his cigarette. "My ex-partner is going through an opera phase now," he said. "He's a weird guy. He was big into black cinema and now he's flirting with opera."

"Then what happened?" DeNafria asked.

"Huh?"

"What you want to be next? After a rock star drummer."

"Oh," Pavlik said. "A ladies' man. And I thought the police force was the road to it."

DeNafria stretched his neck from side to side in the recliner. "And?"

"I found a lady," Pavlik said. He held up a finger. "One. The one for me. The one I wanted to spend the rest of my life with. So we got married and a few years later she dumped me. The one I told you about. Mrs. Pavlik, the first and only. It wasn't in the cards."

DeNafria lit a cigarette. "I pretty much stayed with wanting to be a baseball player," he said. "I was pretty good in high school. I had a few tryout offers for major league teams. The Red Sox, Braves, and Tigers. But then I found the one for me, too. And somebody suggested taking the police test and before I knew it, I could afford to get married, so I did."

"What about Tom Waits?" Pavlik asked.

DeNafria was confused. "Huh?"

"Tom Waits," Pavlik repeated. "He's one of the most talented guys in the world, you ask me. Can write a saloon song or love ballad or just about anything better than anybody. And he's got this voice you can feel when you hear it, you know what I mean?"

DeNafria had lost his place. He squinted. When Pavlik remained silent, he said, "Then Vincent came along. And I had the perfect life."

"I was trying to change the subject here," Pavlik said.

"What, only you get to cry the blues?" DeNafria asked.

Pavlik sipped more of his drink. "Hey, be my guest," he said. "Keep whining."

DeNafria took a long drag on his cigarette. "Thank you," he said as he exhaled.

Pavlik raised his glass in a toast.

Once Pavlik left, DeNafria was drinking straight sour mash from the bottle. His vision was blurred. The room hadn't started to spin yet but he could feel that it wouldn't be long before he was sick. He could feel his head starting to pound from the drinking. When the telephone rang, DeNafria struggled to answer it.

"Hello?" he half-yelled into the phone.

"John?" a feminine voice asked.

"Hello?" DeNafria repeated.

"John, is that you?" the woman asked again.

It took him a few seconds to gather himself. "Jody?" he finally asked.

"Are you alright?" his wife asked him.

"Jody?" he repeated.

"Are you drinking?" she asked.

"Yeah," he said. "Yeah, Jody, I'm drinking."

"Why?"

He coughed on his end. "I want to be drunk."

"I don't appreciate you watching me," she said.

He didn't answer at first.

"John?"

"Huh?"

"I don't want you to watch me. I know it was you. When you sped away, I saw you. That isn't fair."

"I love you, Jody."

"I know you do, John."

"You're my wife."

"I know."

"I miss you."

"I know, but we're separated now."

DeNafria coughed. "Huh?"

"We're separated," his wife said. "You shouldn't come around like that."

"I'm really drunk, Jody."

"I can tell."

DeNafria coughed again. "Huh?" he said.

"Are you alright?"

"Yeah. I'm fine."

"Why don't you sleep it off?"

"I will."

"I'll call you in the morning."

"Will you?"

"Yes."

"Promise?"

"Yes, I promise."

"Alright."

"Good night."

"I love you."

"Good night, John."

"Yeah, right."

When he hung up the phone, he downed two inches of sour mash. He swallowed, belched, lurched forward and vomited on his living room floor.

Aelish was stretching on the living room floor. The pug, Natasha, was sleeping on a pillow on the floor nearby. Aelish had just run seven miles. Her hair was wet with sweat.

Pavlik stood in the doorway with a bag of Chinese food. He had a silly smile on his face. He gawked as Aelish leaned forward between her legs to stretch. "Warming down or up?" he asked.

"If you mean for you, love, it would be up," Aelish said. She bent at the waist, leaned forward, held her position a few seconds and relaxed again.

Pavlik brought the food to the kitchen. He stumbled and banged his right shoulder against the doorway leading to the kitchen.

Aelish sniffed the air about her when she stood up. "Have you been drinking, love?" she asked.

"Somewhat," Pavlik said from the kitchen.

He opened the containers of food and took a chair at one head of the table. The table had already been set. He spooned out beef lo mein into two dishes. He opened a small container of hot mustard and poured some on his lo mein. When Natasha smelled the food, the pug hustled inside the kitchen as well.

"I hope you intend to work some of that off," Aelish said from the kitchen doorway.

Pavlik was clearly disoriented. "Huh?" he said.

Aelish retrieved two cans of Coke from the refrigerator. "For the love of Jesus, man," she said. "I hope you weren't drunk on the job."

When Aelish passed him to set the Cokes on the table, Pavlik reached out and grabbed her. "Nice ass," he said.

Aelish swung at him with the towel she had draped around her neck. "Frisky are we?" she said. She took her seat at the opposite end of the table. "And how was your drunken day?" she asked as she opened her can of soda. "Hit anybody else?"

Pavlik forked a piece of beef from his dish and dropped it on the floor for the pug. "My partner is going through it," he said. "Losing his wife. We saw her with another guy today."

Aelish was surprised. "We?"

Pavlik spoke between bites of lo mein. His speech was some-times slurred. "It was an accident, at least on my part," he said. "I think he was stalking her."

"Stalking? Sounds dangerous. Be careful."

"I think it was her first boyfriend since they split," Pavlik said just before belching. "Which is a good sign they won't be getting back. Which will be the really tough part for him. He's one of those family guineas. Picture albums. Names his kid after his father. Still loves his wife. You know, into it."

Aelish twirled noodles around her fork. "That sounds like a good quality to me," she said. "That he's into his family."

Pavlik dropped another piece of beef onto the floor for the pug. "I don't mean to sound negative about it," he said. He reached for his glass of water. "This mustard is hot."

"Well, don't give it to the dog, man," Aelish said. She waited for him to drink his water. "You don't mean to sound negative but?" she asked.

Pavlik spotted a glob of mustard in the noodles and mixed the concoction with his fork. "Huh?" he said. "Oh, he's not dealing with the reality of the thing. He's whining. He's using the kid to hang around his wife." He stopped to belch again. "He's obvious. Don't get me wrong, I feel bad for the guy. But I know what he's going through. It won't work. All the excess anxiety won't do anything for him. In the end she'll take off with this guy we saw her with or some other guy. What's the difference?"

"Aren't you the psychologist," Aelish said. She wiped her mouth with a paper napkin. She watched Pavlik wipe his mouth with the back of his wrist and handed him a napkin.

Pavlik belched loud this time. "Thanks," he said.

"That was attractive," Aelish said. "Do you think he'll do any-thing foolish, your partner?"

Pavlik took a deep breath. "I don't think so," he said. "But who knows. He's sure into his kid. Who knows how he'll react if she decides to get serious with somebody. I went home with him. Got him started on the exorcism of the evil spirit of his wife. Hopefully he'll get drunk, throw up his guts and he won't be able to think about it tomorrow."

Aelish laughed. "Doctor Pavlik, I presume," she said.

"Father Pavlik," he corrected her. "I'm the senior detective, thank you. Some of the lads come to me for counseling from time to time. I'm rather priestly, if I do say so myself."

"Excuse me," Aelish said. "You a priest? Aren't we all in for it. I don't think so, love. You're a lot of things probably but a priest is hardly one of them."

"Well, I know what to do with guys in situations like this," Pavlik said. He fed the dog another piece of his beef.

"Get them drunk, yes, of course," Aelish said. "How original."

Pavlik opened, then raised his can of soda. "Sometimes that's all a guy needs, a good stiff one," he said.

Aelish shot him a wink. "Sometimes that's all a girl needs, too," she said.

Pavlik coughed from choking on his soda.

Chapter 23

The sun was just starting to rise. The street was quiet except for a woman walking a poodle along Avenue T. Jack Fama knocked on the front door of 2186, Coyle Street. Fama was dressed in a black nylon warm-up suit. He wore dark sunglasses and kept his back to the street.

"Who is it?" a tired voice asked.

"Police," Fama said.

The door locks turned and Fama opened the screen door. The wood door opened a crack and Fama pushed his way inside the home. A frail woman with gray hair was knocked to the green-and-white checkered linoleum floor. The woman gasped from the fall. She grabbed at her right hip.

Fama stepped further inside the kitchen and grabbed the end of the woman's pink nightgown. He pulled it up over her head as he dragged her under the table.

"Hey!" a voice yelled from further back in the house. "What you do there!"

Fama looked up and saw the old man running toward him.

"You get the hell out of here!" the old man was saying. "What you do my wife?"

The old man pushed Fama away from the table and kneeled down to cover his wife.

Fama pointed a finger at the old man. "Jimmy wants his money," he said. "You have it the next time I find you, old man."

"Get the fuck out of here!" the old man was yelling. "Get out!"

Fama smiled. "I'll be back," he said.

The old man ran for the telephone. "I call the cops," he said.

Fama shoved the old man away from the telephone. He pulled a black stiletto from his jacket pocket and cut the telephone wire. He waved the knife at the old man a few times before retracting the blade and leaving the house. Fama could hear the old woman crying behind him as he slammed the door shut.

He let himself in with the key he kept for when he stopped over. He had watched the front of the building from the backseat of a taxi parked two hundred yards from the front lobby. He had watched Jimmy Mangino leave. He had waited an extra ten minutes wondering what he would do. When the taxi driver finally asked him how long they would be there, Larry Berra handed the man a crisp fifty-dollar bill and slid off the backseat.

Now he was in the living room of the apartment. The early sun was shining bright through the living room windows. Berra could hear the television in the bedroom. He made his way slowly into the doorway of the bedroom. When his shadow crossed her bed, Leanna gasped from the sight.

"Jesus Christ, you scared the shit out of me," she said. She had just come out of the shower and was sitting against the backboard in a white cotton robe with a towel wrapped around her head. She leaned forward on her knees from being frightened.

"What are you doing here?" Leanna asked.

"I saw him," Berra said. He lit a cigarette. "I saw him leave downstairs."

"What did you expect," Leanna said. "I know what you said about me."

"Did you blow him?" Berra asked. "That what he came by for?"

"No," Leanna said.

Berra was glaring into her eyes. "You fuck him?"

"No."

"Bullshit."

"I didn't. So, stop it."

Berra leaned against the doorframe. "I can't believe you did this to me."

"To you?" Leanna said. "What I did to you? How about what you did to me? What you called me in front of that ape. I'm a piece of ass. I'm just another cunt. Thanks, Larry, for all the good fucking times we had. So much for that, huh?"

Berra frowned. "I have to talk like that with guys like Mangino," he said.

"Yeah, well, you talk too much, Larry," Leanna said. "I was supposed to be your girlfriend. You're supposed to respect me for that. I mean, how do you think you sound, talking about the woman you're with like that? You sound cheap, Larry. Like you're just another asshole."

Berra had tears in his eyes. "You're so fucking beautiful, Leanna," he said. "It kills me that you slept with him."

Leanna looked down.

Berra's bottom lip was quivering. "Why?" he asked her. "Why?"

"I didn't want to, Larry," Leanna finally said. "I hate him."

"Then why? Why the fuck did you do it?"

"Because he told me what you said about me," Leanna said. "He came here and he told me and I was angry at you. I had a few drinks with him and that was that. I'm not even sure I'm sorry. I don't like him but I don't know that I can ever like you again. He's not the one who called me a cunt, Larry."

"I still love you," Berra said. He was crying.

Leanna made a face. "How can you say that?"

"I do."

"I think you should leave."

Larry was sniffling. "I don't want to leave," he said.

"I think you have to. I don't want to start something again. I don't think I can ever put that behind me, what you called me. He's out to get you, that animal. He's out to get you but you took his word against me. And you betrayed me with him. I can't forget that."

Larry stopped sniffling. "What do you mean he's out to get me?"

"The money," Leanna said. "What you accuse me of, I'm sure."

Larry grabbed what little hair he had left. "Shit," he said. "Fuck."

Leanna watched his dramatics from the middle of the bed. When he was sitting on the edge of the bed and crying into his hands, she moved closer to him. She took his head and held it against her chest. She frowned as she kissed his forehead.

"Don't leave me," Larry said.

"I won't," Leanna said.

"Please," Larry said.

Leanna kissed his head as she rolled her eyes. "I won't," she repeated.

It was nearly noon before Larry Berra left Leanna's apartment.

She watched the street below from her living room window until she saw Berra get inside a taxi. As soon as the taxi drove away from the curb, Leanna called the beeper number on the identification card her latest boyfriend had given her.

"Someone page me?" George Wilson asked when Leanna answered the return phone call.

"How soon you forget," Leanna told Wilson.

"Hot stuff!" Wilson said.

"I have a recording," Leanna said.

"Good for you."

"Yes, it is. Both of them. One after the other."

"Did they say anything worth recording?"

"One told me I was his alibi."

"Which one was that?"

"The real gangster."

"Alibi for what?"

"He didn't say."

"And the other one? What did he have to say?"

"He begged me not to dump him."

"That doesn't sound too sinister."

"I told you, he's the harmless one."

"Do you want me to file this tape with the task force?"

"With the who?"

"The organized crime task force. It could mean you'd have to testify someday."

"Couldn't I just file it with you?"

"What good would that do?"

"In case I don't want to use it. Or I want to use it at a later time. Couldn't I do that?"

"It wouldn't be official. I couldn't ask anyone to act on your behalf unless it is. The police, for instance."

"But you would hold it, just in case."

"I guess I could be persuaded."

"You guess?"

"Where are you now?"

"Home but I haven't slept all night. And the real gangster is picking me up later. He has a surprise for me, he said."

"Are you going to tape him again?"

"Of course. Why wouldn't I?"

"Because he's not the harmless one."

"I can handle him."

"It's your call. What time is he picking you up?"

"Late afternoon. Why?"

"I could be at the gym before two."

"I'll be asleep."

"I can wake you."

"I'll leave a key at the front desk."

"Should I be gentle or rough?"

"When you wake me or fuck me?"

"Either."

"Surprise me."

Chapter 24

Aelish had watched Pavlik during the night. The nightmares from finding the boys were still haunting him. His restless sleep was getting worse. He was talking in his sleep. He was yelling. He was reaching for something or somebody.

They had been asleep less than two hours when he first started to stir in the bed. Aelish didn't wake him. He had broken out in a sweat. He had mumbled something about a boy. He had turned from side to side with his teeth clenched tight. He had held up his hands, his fingers spread, and suddenly dropped his arms and he was calm again.

Aelish had applied a wet towel to his forehead when he was calm. When he was peacefully asleep again, she lay on her side and watched him. She had just closed her own eyes when it started again.

It took longer this time before Pavlik was resting again. He had nearly fallen off the bed from his twisting. He had nearly hit her with a punch he had thrown at the air. Aelish was exhausted when his fit was over. After another hour of watching him, she finally fell asleep. When she woke up again, Pavlik was no longer in the bed.

She listened for the shower. It was the way he usually woke himself from the nightmares. He would let the water run cold a long time before he stepped under the shower. He would stand still under the water until he couldn't feel the cold. Then he would pat himself dry and sit in his chair in the living room a long while. He would sit silent with his eyes closed until he couldn't see the haunting images anymore. That's what he had told her. The images of the boys, the dead boy and the one he had saved, haunted him.

Aelish tiptoed through the apartment until she saw him sitting in the chair. He had earphones on. He seemed to be mouthing the words to a song. She crept up behind him and tried to listen.

"*No, no, principessa altera,*" Pavlik was whisper-singing. "*Tu volgio tutto ardente d'amore.*"

She touched his shoulder gently. He stopped the portable CD player he was using.

"What does it mean, love?" she asked him.

"It's from an opera," he said. "*Turandot.* Puccini." He took her hand as Aelish sat on the couch near his chair. "It's the prince's response to the princess after he wins his right to marry her. He solves these riddles, for which he could lose his head should he get them wrong. But he doesn't. He answers the three riddles and she has to marry him, but she doesn't want to. She's not a very nice character, if you know the story, but he's in love with her and she asks him 'would you take me by force?' and he responds with that, '*No, no, principessa.*' It means, 'No, proud princess. I will have you aflame with love.' Something like that."

"It's pretty," Aelish said.

Pavlik had tears in his eyes. "I couldn't sleep again," he said.

"I know, love," she said. She tightened her hold on his hands. "I was with you."

They sat in silence a while. The pug, Natasha, appeared in the bedroom doorway.

"What do you want?" Pavlik asked the dog.

Its small corkscrew tail immediately started to wag. The dog crossed the room and lay at Pavlik's feet. He reached down to scratch its stomach.

"What a life, huh?" Pavlik asked.

"Now that you saved her," Aelish said.

Pavlik turned to Aelish. "You're not sore anymore about that? How I got her."

"I never was sore about that, man," Aelish said. "I was just pointing out that you might be losing control of your temper a wee bit. You did the right thing. Natasha didn't belong with someone who'd kick her. No dog deserves that. No animal deserves that."

Pavlik swallowed hard. "When my parents first broke up," he said. "I lived with my mother. She used to kick our dog like that. She'd get drunk and bring men home and get nasty with everything."

Aelish kissed one of his hands.

"I ran away a couple times," he said. "I kept running away until my father took me in. He was a cop, too."

"You're a good man, Alex," Aelish said. "You know you are."

He sniffled. He wiped his nose with the back of his free wrist. "I don't know if I can get over it," he said. "What I saw. Those kids, I mean. What I saw when I was a kid."

"You can get help," Aelish said.

"I don't know that I can."

"You have to. I'll help you."

The dog had turned completely onto its back. It whined when Pavlik stopped scratching its belly.

Pavlik was looking into Aelish's eyes then. He told her, "I love you, honey."

"And I love you," Aelish said.

The dog whined again and they both said, "Shhhh."

The stench in the apartment nearly made him sick again. He opened all the windows and dropped to his hands and knees to scrub at the vomit stains on his rug. DeNafria gagged more than a few times while he attempted to clean the mess he had made.

He had slept less than five hours. His head was pounding from the dehydration of a bad drunk. He popped a handful of Tylenol and forced himself to drink two full glasses of water. He took a long hot shower and scrubbed himself.

Once he was satisfied with the rug and the breeze blowing through the open windows, DeNafria took a walk around the block to clear his head. It was still early morning. The sun had yet to dawn. Except for an occasional car, the streets were still.

DeNafria walked the length of the park across Eighty-sixth Street. After a while he recognized a man sitting on a bench.

"Father John?" DeNafria said.

The man looked up from behind a newspaper. He was a short, heavy man. His hair was curly gray. He squinted at DeNafria until he started to smile.

"Son of a bitch," the man said. "Johnny DeNafria." He folded his newspaper and stood up. He reached out and grabbed DeNafria's right hand. He shook it vigorously.

"Son of a bitch?" DeNafria said. "Is that any way for a priest to talk?"

"Don't break 'em, kid," the priest said. "I don't have my collar on, I'm just another angry Knicks fan the day after they lost another easy one. The Cleveland Cavaliers, for God's sake. How the hell are you?"

DeNafria gave his best effort at a genuine smile for the priest. "I've been better," he said. "You would catch me the day after a bad drunk."

The priest took his seat on the bench again. He patted the bench beside him for DeNafria to sit. "How's the family?" the priest asked.

DeNafria sat on the bench obediently. "We're split up," he said.

The priest winced as if in pain. "Oh, I'm sorry to hear that, John. Truly, I am. Are you okay?"

DeNafria shrugged. "I'm dealing."

"Sometimes it helps to talk about these things," the priest said. "If you want to, I've nothing better to do."

"I think the time has come for me to accept things," DeNafria said. "You know how it goes. One day at a time."

The priest let the moment pass. "How's your mom?" he asked.

"Fine, thanks," DeNafria said. "She's a tough broad. She'll outlive the lot of us."

"Do you see your boy?" the priest asked. "Is everything smooth with visitations?"

"I still have Vincent, Father, yes," DeNafria said. "It isn't a total loss."

The priest pointed to the sky. "This used to be my favorite time of the day," he said. He pointed up and down Eighty-sixth Street. "The traffic kind of spoils it now. It seems to start earlier and earlier. I come out here to read my paper, frustrate myself with the local teams and so on. But I usually wait for the sunrises. I enjoy the sunrise more and more lately."

"I can't remember being up this early," DeNafria said.

"Try it sometime," the priest said. "Waking up early, I mean. Just to see a sunrise. It clears the mind, looking at something that beautiful. For me, it reminds me just how magnificent God really is. It may remind you about your boy, how magnificent he is, to still have him, no matter what happens between you and Jody."

DeNafria pointed to a delicatessen off the far corner. "How about a coffee, Father? On me."

The priest waved at the offer. "I said you should try getting up early. I've been up for hours. Drank half a pot already. Thanks but no thanks. The next thing I drink this morning will be a nice shot of wine. I serve the eight o'clock mass."

"I remember serving the seven-thirty mass," DeNafria said.

"Imagine that," the priest said. "You were an altar boy. Christ we must have been desperate back then."

"I hear it's worse today," DeNafria said. "Girls serving mass."

The priest made a face. "Take a good look in the mirror, John," he said. "You're a handsome man but I'd rather look at a pretty woman any day of the week. Sorry to say, of course."

"You sure about the coffee?" DeNafria asked. "I have to get back home. I left half the place wide open. The windows."

"Couldn't handle your booze, eh?" the priest teased.

"It's been a while since I was drunk," DeNafria said. "Since my bachelor party, I think."

"Not me," the priest said. "Man's got to tie one on every now and then. It was just last week, in fact. Between the late mass and a formal dinner at the rectory and a few shots watching the Knicks game. I was stinking pretty bad when I closed my eyes."

DeNafria patted the priest on the back. "You're a pistol, Father John," he said.

"A pistol?" the priest asked.

"Yeah," DeNafria said. He winked at his old friend. "I'll see you around."

The priest pointed at DeNafria. "Not if I see you first," he said.

Chapter 25

When DeNafria finally caught up with Pavlik again, it was in the late afternoon and the rain had just started to fall. Pavlik was parked outside the Coney Island social club where Joe Sharpetti's crew spent their spare time playing cards.

DeNafria parked his minivan directly behind the department issued Ford Taurus the detectives had been using. Pavlik's jaw was tight when DeNafria sat up front with him.

"You got the call?" Pavlik asked DeNafria.

"From the old man, yeah," DeNafria said. "She's alright. Bruised but alright. Did you show her the mug shots?"

"I brought them to her," Pavlik said. "She picked out this slick fuck, Fama."

"It wasn't Mangino?"

"No. What's the difference?"

DeNafria pointed up the block. "You want to go in and arrest him?"

"That's why I called you."

"Let's do it."

Both men were out of the car in an instant. As they walked the half-block toward the social club, DeNafria said, "There'll be plenty of witnesses in there. Not to mention federal wiretaps. Maybe some cameras."

"What's your point?" Pavlik asked.

"No hands," DeNafria said. "Not in front of people. Especially inside. Like I said, it'll probably be recorded. Not to mention whoever is wearing a wire in there."

Pavlik stopped dead in his tracks.

"What?" DeNafria said.

"Maybe we should wait for him out here," Pavlik said.

DeNafria thought about it a second. He said, "Maybe you're right."

Vittorio Tangorra had Larry Berra paged in his apartment by the concierge at the front desk of the Corinthian Condominiums on First Avenue. The old man stood in the huge marble lobby and measured the security. Besides the concierge and the doorman, there were several security cameras hung from various locations around the ceiling lobby. Tangorra touched the .25mm in his right pants pocket nervously when he realized he was standing in the direct view of a ceiling camera.

After a few minutes, the concierge pointed to the banks of elevators further back in the lobby.

"To the right," the concierge said. "Thirtieth floor. Thirty-I."

Tangorra nodded at the concierge and slowly made his way toward the elevators. He kept his head tucked down to avoid the cameras aimed at the elevators.

Leanna was dressed in a short white skirt, a tight yellow pullover top and white high heels. She sat on the edge of a queen-size bed in an airport motel room. Her long brown hair was tied in a ponytail. She had just applied a fresh coat of lipstick when the second Quaalude kicked in. Her vision turned blurry as she fumbled in an attempt to lean back on her hands.

"Holy shhhit," she said.

Mangino spoke in whispers with the fat man in the next room. The door between the adjacent rooms was ajar.

"Who'd you get?" Mangino asked.

"The two young guys," the fat man said. "The black guys are in L.A. auditioning for the big leagues."

"These kids alright?"

"They're fine. All they're here for is the money."

"Okay, then," Mangino said. He had already pulled his wallet out. He removed ten one hundred dollar bills. "Five hundred each, right?"

The fat man took the money and stashed it inside his front pants pocket. He was wearing beige shorts and a black Old Navy sweatshirt.

"And you're doing the camera?" Mangino asked. "Don't forget, I need a few copies."

The fat man held up two fingers. "Two handheld cameras," he said. "Nancy, my wife, is coming. She's stopping on her way over to pick up the other camera."

Mangino held both his hands up. "No extra cost, I hope."

The fat man made a face. "For fun," he said. "What's wrong with you?"

"Right," Mangino said. "What is wrong with me."

DeNafria flashed his badge and identification. "Jack Fama?" he asked.

Fama looked from one detective to the other. "What you want?" Fama asked them.

Pavlik grabbed the gangster by the arms and turned him toward a parked car. He shoved hard and the gangster slammed against the side door of a Cadillac Seville.

"You're under arrest for breaking and entering and assault," DeNafria said.

"What the fuck is this?" Fama yelled.

Pavlik lifted Fama's elbows and the gangster grunted. "You have the right to shut the fuck up," Pavlik said. "Or I'll push a little harder and your elbows will be where your shoulders are."

DeNafria looked up and down the street before opening the back passenger door of the Ford Taurus. Pavlik shoved Fama hard into the backseat. Fama's forehead struck the roof of the car and split enough to bleed.

"Ouch!" Fama yelled. "Watch it, motherfucker!"

Pavlik threw a quick jab into Fama's belly and flung the mobster across the backseat. "Careful getting in," he said.

DeNafria wedged his way between Pavlik and Fama. He pointed to the front seat. "You drive," he told Pavlik.

"Vittorio! Come in, come in," Larry Berra said. He was groggy from sleeping. He wore a white monogrammed cotton robe and matching slippers. A thick gold chain dangled in his chest hairs.

Vittorio Tangorra looked around immediately as he stepped inside the luxury apartment. His right hand was glued to the .25mm in his right pants pocket.

Berra tried to drape an arm around Tangorra's shoulders but the old man pulled away fast.

"Easy, easy," Berra said. "I'm just being nice. Would you like some coffee?"

"Who you send to my house?" Tangorra asked.

"Huh?" Berra said. "Send who?"

"This morning," Tangorra said. "Somebody come into my house. Into my house!"

Berra put both his hands up. "Easy, Vittorio, easy," he said. "I swear on my mother, I didn't send nobody."

Tangorra's face was taut. "He throw my wife down on the floor," Tangorra said through clenched teeth. "He pull her nightgown over her head. He shove her. He shove me. In my house!"

Berra was shaking his head. "It had to be Jimmy Bench-Press," he said. "On his own, I swear." He raised his right hand up as he covered his heart with his left hand.

"You full of shit," Tangorra said.

Berra was still shaking his head. "No, Vittorio, I'm not full of shit. I swear. I already called those cops. I'm supposed to meet them. They have to get back to me."

Tangorra stood staring. After a few seconds, he pulled the .25mm from his front pants pocket and pointed it at Berra. Berra's eyes opened wide as he backpedaled until he fell to the floor.

One of the two boys shooting the scene found the recorder in Leanna's red leather pocketbook while she lay semiconscious on the bed. Mangino removed the mini-cassette tape from the device and replaced it with a blank tape. He replaced the recording device inside the pocketbook and enjoyed the show on the bed in front of him.

Both boys were seventeen-years-old. Both had been doing

porn for more than a year. They positioned Leanna so her legs were up high as one of the boys lay between them. The other boy kneeled behind her on the bed and tried to force himself in her mouth. The fat man and his wife focused their cameras up close. When the fat man said "Action," the boy lying between Leanna's legs penetrated her.

Leanna gagged at first from the boy forcing himself in her mouth. Her head turned to one side but the boy quickly held her head steady. She tried to speak and he was inside her mouth. She moaned once or twice before her eyes closed and she lay mostly limp.

Chapter 26

John Feller watched with detectives DeNafria and Pavlik as Jack Fama was escorted out of the Brooklyn general lockup. They were inside an interrogation room looking through a one-way mirror. Fama's forehead sported a fresh gauze bandage. He ducked his head, as he was led out of the lockup pen.

"This is bullshit," Pavlik said.

"Deal with it," Feller said.

DeNafria tried to signal Pavlik to let it go.

"What?" Pavlik said.

"The guy is with us," Feller said. "Which is something you shouldn't know but now you do. Sometimes this stuff happens, there's nothing you can do about it. This is obviously one of those times. But now both of you have information that can compromise a witness against the mob, which is a federal violation, not to mention a crime in itself."

"Blow me," Pavlik said.

"Thanks, but no thanks," Feller said. He was holding a manila envelope. He opened it and handed DeNafria four pictures of Fama being arrested earlier.

"Yeah, so?" DeNafria said to Feller. "We arrested him. We know that."

Pavlik grabbed the pictures from DeNafria.

"You notice the bandage on his forehead just before?" Feller asked.

"He hit his head," DeNafria said. "He isn't the first guy managed that."

Feller pointed to the pictures Pavlik was still looking over. "Those are stills made from a surveillance tape," Feller said. "We saw how Fama was shoved. We saw the punch Detective Pavlik issued. We saw how Fama managed seven stitches getting into the back of a car with handcuffs on."

Pavlik dropped the pictures on a table. "You see him shove the old lady?" he asked.

Feller yawned. "No, we didn't," he said.

"Well, she filled out a complaint," Pavlik said. "She picked his face from a set of mug shots."

"What about it?" DeNafria asked. "It was an old lady he shoved around."

"We'll take it into consideration," Feller said.

Pavlik stroked the air up and down with a fist.

"More or less," Feller said.

"We also have an ongoing investigation," DeNafria said.

Feller held up a hand. "Trust me, ours is bigger than yours," he said.

Pavlik was biting his lower lip. "Just like that, huh?" he said.

"There's always a chance your charges against Fama will stick," Feller said. "I'm not saying it's a complete wash. But they will have to take a backseat to what he's doing for us and there is always the chance your charges will be dropped at some future time. We're after the bigger fish in this thing, guys. This is how it works."

Pavlik shook his head at DeNafria. "Translation," he said. "Dirtbags in the witness protection program have immunity to commit violent crimes."

"He did beat up an old lady," DeNafria reminded Feller.

"He knocked her down," Feller said.

"Maybe it should have been your mother," Pavlik said.

"My mother is dead," Feller said back. Now he was glaring at Pavlik.

"Look," DeNafria said. "You can't blame us for being pissed about this. Aside from what he did, we just wasted a lot of time and energy chasing him for nothing."

Feller didn't respond.

"Right," Pavlik said.

Larry Berra had stained himself when Vittorio Tangorra fired the .25mm at the wall. He watched as the old man quickly panicked and fled the apartment. Berra remained in shock at least an hour after the incident. He didn't clean himself until the telephone surprised him.

"Do you still love her?" Jimmy Mangino asked Berra when he answered the phone.

Berra measured his response. "I don't know. Why?"

"Because I have a tape," Mangino said.

Berra made a face. "A what?"

"A tape. A VCR tape. I'll drop it off at your front desk. It's pretty crude, though. You better be sitting when you watch it."

Berra was squinting. "You and her?" he asked nervously.

"Worse," Mangino told him. "A lot worse. It's something I

wouldn't think you'd want floating around the city. Not with the company we keep."

"I don't understand," Berra said.

"Take a look at the thing and you'll understand fast enough," Mangino said.

Berra was shaking his head. "Why would I care?" he asked.

Mangino laughed. "Reputation, for one thing," he said. "Appearances. I mean, it's bad enough half the guys on the street crack jokes about the fifty-eight grand you gave some barber. Imagine the conversations when it gets out your girl is making porn flicks."

Berra's head snapped back. "Porn flicks?"

"Leanna does the college circuit," Mangino said. "Like Debbie did Dallas."

Berra held the phone away from him a second. When he put it back against his ear, Mangino said, "Larry? You still there?"

"Yeah, I'm here," Berra answered.

"It's expensive, the movie she made."

"How expensive?"

"One hundred grand," Mangino said. "The first fifty of which is due pronto. I can reach out for you on this, try and recover some of the money you lay out but it'll still cost. Some big shots will have to go to work fast here. They require compensation. Bring fifty-K to your friend Benny for starters. He'll know what to do."

Berra took a deep breath. "Benny is in on this?" he asked.

"In on what, Larry?" Mangino asked back. "You're getting all paranoid. We're all trying to help you here. Don't get in our way."

Berra was silent again.

"Larry?"

"Yeah."

"Go get the money."

When Leanna finally woke up, she was alone in a motel room she vaguely remembered. She was naked except for her thong underwear, which were on backward. Her clothes had been dropped over the back of a folding chair.

It took her several minutes to compose herself. When she tried to stand, she felt pain in her groin and anus. She made her way into the bathroom and attempted to clean herself in the shower. Leanna wiped herself with a tissue and saw she had been bleeding.

She started to cry at her reflection in the mirror when she remembered her tape recorder and George Wilson's business card. She looked inside her purse and found a VCR tape with Wilson's business card attached. She pulled the business card off the tape and saw there was writing on the back of the card.

"Nice try, cunt," it read.

Leanna gasped, held her breath a few seconds, then let out a bloodcurdling scream.

Chapter 27

Commissioner Robert Downs was looking at the four still shots of the arrest of Jack Fama in his office when Michael McDonald entered the room. It had been a busy day for Downs. There had been five murders in total the night before in New York City's five boroughs.

Downs motioned at the two chairs directly in front of his desk. McDonald took the chair to the right. Downs handed the pictures to McDonald across the desk. McDonald squinted to see.

"It's Pavlik and DeNafria," Downs said. "Our two golden boys. The one shoving the perp into the car is Pavlik. He split the guy's forehead. Seven stitches."

McDonald examined the pictures closer. "Where did these come from?"

"The guys so eager to cooperate with us," Downs said. "The Effa-bee-eye. It was their surveillance caught this."

"Did the guy bring charges?" McDonald asked. "I would think not if he's working with the feds."

Downs shook his head. "No, he didn't, not the perp," he said. "Like I said, the FBI sent me this tape. Either the agent in charge has a personal hard-on for our detectives or he's a beacon of light and justice for all. The point is, I won't let this go any further and you and your boss have nothing to say about it."

McDonald was squinting again. "Meaning?"

"I'm calling in our marker," Downs said. "You owe the city one and now I'm calling it in. Specifically, early retirement for these two. Before it gets embarrassing and we can't stop it from going to press."

McDonald held up his hands. "Both of them?" he said. "That sounds like two favors to me. I'm not even sure I can deliver one of them."

"Oh, you can alright," Downs said. "I'll make sure of that."

McDonald took a long deep breath. "I can only take one of them out," he said. "Not the both of them." He pointed at the pictures. "And from here, it doesn't look like DeNafria had anything to do with this."

Downs stared McDonald down. McDonald ignored the staring contest. "One," McDonald said. "Not both of them."

"Fine," Downs said after a while. "Pavlik. Make him retire."

"What about his compensation?" McDonald asked.

"We'll work that out," Downs said. "Full benefits, except for overtime accumulation. No bonuses for this guy. He can forget that perk."

"That isn't fair," McDonald said.

"Life isn't fair," Downs said. "Especially you let yourself get out of control."

"How about half the overtime accumulation?" McDonald offered.

"None," Downs said. "Flat salary or nothing, we suspend and put him through a departmental trial."

McDonald nodded. Downs backed his chair away from his desk.

"I see things going from worse to scandal here," Downs said. "The man is out of control. He had to know there was surveillance on that block. It's a known mob hangout."

"What if he doesn't want out?" McDonald asked.

"Make him want it," Downs said. "Explain that thing about jail for assaulting Timothy Waller again. Explain how he's building a pattern of such behavior. Explain how much the city urges him to retire."

"This may not fly the way you think," McDonald said. "One day a gold shield hero, the next month the same guy has had enough, he's retiring. For what? How do we explain that one to the press?"

"Stress," Downs said without emotion. "From finding a dead little boy. From finding the one he saved. From dealing with the dirtbags in organized crime. Take your pick."

McDonald held up the pictures. "What about these?" he asked.

"Use them to influence Pavlik if you have to," Downs said. "Then do what comes natural, Mike."

"You mean burn them," McDonald said.

"Use them to roast marshmallows," Downs said. "Have a picnic, you and your boss."

Both detectives stopped at their makeshift office in a one-bedroom apartment, sometimes used by the organized crime unit, in Brooklyn Heights. They had just finished drinking coffee. Pavlik used the bathroom while DeNafria spoke to his wife on the phone. When Pavlik was finished in the bathroom, he heard DeNafria hang up the phone.

"Can you sit in for me?" DeNafria asked. "My wife just called about my son. She thinks he broke his arm."

"Sure," Pavlik said. "He alright?"

"He's probably fine but I want to be there," DeNafria said.

Pavlik pointed to the door. "Sure, go ahead."

"You sure you're alright?" DeNafria asked. "I can try and get Berra and postpone this until later."

Pavlik was confused. "Doesn't this guy know who you are?" he asked. "I may spook him, no?"

"No," DeNafria said. "We spoke on the phone for less than a minute. I made the original appointment through the old man, Vittorio. As far as Larry Berra is concerned, I'm you."

"If you say so," Pavlik said.

"Berra sounded scared," DeNafria said. "Either they're making a move on him or he's into trouble we don't know about. Drugs maybe. Maybe he financed something else he has no business in. Who knows. Maybe he's about to get pinched. Just the thought of doing jail time would make Berra flip."

Pavlik smiled.

DeNafria smiled back. "You like it when the bad guys start to fold, huh?"

"This may work out after all," Pavlik said, still smiling.

"Try not to hit him," DeNafria said.

"Excuse me?" Pavlik said as he lost his smile.

"It was a joke," DeNafria said.

Mangino had been told to dress up and be ready for a party shortly before sunset. He had asked Rosemary DiCicco to help him with his tie after she had finished giving him a blow job in his temporary room in her basement. She had given Mangino the same tie she claimed her husband had worn the night they were married.

Mangino stopped at a local bar and called Leanna Flynn. He told her the price he had asked Larry Berra to pay for the remaining copies of the pornographic tape they had made of her. He laughed when she started to scream at him.

"It's not like you won't get anything," he told Leanna. "Twenty percent is better than nothing."

Leanna hung up on him.

He was picked up at the bar by Benjamin Luchessi and then dropped off on Knapp Street in Sheepshead Bay. He was escorted onto a private cabin cruiser and formally introduced to men he knew were captains with the Vignieri crime family. Most of the captains left the boat and Mangino was introduced to two other men who were dressed for a party. Mangino and the two men sat on the wraparound bench on the back of the boat and awaited further instructions.

The boat left the dock shortly after sunset. It cruised at a slow but steady speed along the coast of Brooklyn. Mangino recognized the lights off Manhattan Beach and later Coney Island. The three men engaged in mostly small talk and avoided discussing what it was they were there for.

One hour after they had left the dock at Sheepshead Bay, one of the captains who had stayed behind emerged from the cabin. He held the door open and guided the three men into the hull.

The underboss, consigliere, and two captains of the Vignieri crime family sat around an oval table inside the hull. Mangino and the other two men were formally introduced. The underboss of the family stood up at the head of the table and the ceremony that would induct Jimmy Mangino into the Vignieri crime family began.

Chapter 28

Special Agent John Feller examined the videotape at the Sixtieth Precinct on West Eighth Street in Brooklyn. It was a black-and-white security tape of the area directly in front of Eugene Tranchatta's apartment. Part of the walkway leading to the sidewalk, some garbage pails, and the doormat, were visible on the tape. When Jimmy Mangino appeared in the tape, he was heading toward the apartment. He stood in the doorway almost a full minute before the top of the doorframe was visible when it opened. Mangino disappeared from the camera's view immediately after the doorframe disappeared again.

Dexter Greene, the NYPD homicide detective investigating the murder of Eugene Tranchatta, stopped the videotape to note the time. "Three-fifteen A.M.," he said. He started the tape again. "Now he's in."

Agent Feller sipped black coffee from a plastic cup.

Greene let the tape run at normal speed. "I always wanted to be a director," he said. "Black cinema mostly but I like action films, too. Here I'd have him pull his weapon on his way down the path."

"That would be convenient," Feller said.

Greene held up a finger at the agent. He fast-forwarded the tape until Jimmy Mangino appeared in front of the door again.

This time Mangino was heading out of the apartment. He walked briskly down the walkway toward the street.

"Three-eighteen," Detective Greene said. "He's in and out in just under three minutes. One of which he might've been knocking on the door."

"Which isn't good for a case," Feller said. "I could hear his lawyer now: The victim wasn't home."

"Maybe he needs another take," Greene said.

Feller glanced at his watch.

Greene pointed to the screen. "Watch," he said. He rewound the tape to where Mangino was walking toward the apartment. He stopped it when Mangino reached inside the jacket he was wearing. "There," he said. "In scene two you'll notice the perp is reaching for something inside his jacket. Five'll get you ten, it isn't a candy bar for new uniforms for the Police Athletic Little League he's looking to peddle."

"Can you enhance it?" Feller asked.

Greene nodded. "We'll have it tomorrow sometime," he said. "It's a gun. I can make out the handle without enhancement. The guy was found shot in the face. Find the guy, you may find the gun."

"Now you're talking like the Easter bunny," Feller said.

"It happens," Greene said. "Sometimes a guy thinks he's free and clear, he doesn't want to buy another one. I've had that happen before. Professional hit men, no less. Use the same gun more than once and pay the bargain price down the road. Two for the price of one."

"What time tomorrow will you have the enhancement?" Feller asked.

"Afternoon sometime," Greene said. "I'll give you a call."

The door opened and Detective Arlene Belzinger stepped inside. Belzinger was thirty-three, beautiful and tough. She had jet-black, short, straight hair and big brown eyes. Her lips were thick. Her body was tight. She closed the door behind her and held up two separate ballistics reports.

"Same gun killed the two Koreans at the Brooklyn Inn," she said. Her voice was husky.

Feller smiled. "Hello, hello, hello," he said.

Belzinger frowned at Greene.

Greene thumbed at Feller. "Man's a fed," he said. "They don't know any better."

Feller was shifting his eyes toward Belzinger for Greene. "Suddenly I'm very envious of you, Detective."

Greene put on a phony smile. "It's a black thing," he said. "I understands."

"There are no witnesses putting Mangino at the Brooklyn Inn but it's a fifteen minute drive at best from there to Tranchatta's place," Belzinger said. "He had plenty of time to go back and forth, or look for him first."

"Thank you," Feller said.

"This a wrap?" Greene asked.

Feller was still gawking at Belzinger. "Huh?" he said to Greene.

"We done?" Greene asked again.

"Ah, sure, yes," Feller said. He turned to Belzinger. "Unless you have time for a bite for lunch?" he said.

Belzinger faked gagging. "Sorry, 'fraid not," she said.

"Maybe some other time?" Greene offered.

Belzinger forced a sarcastic smile at Greene and exited the room.

"At least she didn't say no," Feller said.

"Trust me," Greene said. "She said, no."

"He's a friend," Jody DeNafria said.

John DeNafria was glaring across the emergency room at the man he had already seen with his wife. It was crowded in the emergency room. Two security guards were standing near the front door.

"You bring him around Vincent?" DeNafria asked his wife. "Is it that fucking easy for you? You just bring him around like that?"

Jody DeNafria took a deep breath. She set her hands firmly on her hips and tried to block her husband's line of sight with her head.

"Stop it!" she yelled. She looked around herself then spoke through clenched teeth. "Talk to me, damn it! Look at me!"

John DeNafria bit his lower lip as he stared down into his wife's eyes. "I don't want him around my kid," he said. "I don't want him around Vincent ever."

"David brought me here," Jody DeNafria said. "He was passing by and he saw me walking with Vincent. He gave us a lift is all."

DeNafria's jaw was tight. "David? That his name?"

"John, please."

"Motherfucker."

"John?"

He tried to move his wife out of the way but she used both hands to block him.

"No!" Jody DeNafria yelled. "Stay here, damn it."

They both stopped fighting a moment. The security guards across the emergency room had turned toward DeNafria and his wife.

DeNafria took a deep breath and glared into his wife's eyes.

"You don't need a lift," he finally said. "You have a fucking car I pay for, remember? You have me. I'm Vincent's father, damn it."

His wife shook her head. "You have to stop this," she said.

DeNafria turned toward the wall and slammed a fist into it. His wife grabbed both his arms and held onto him.

"Stop it, damn you!" she said. "You're making a fucking scene."

DeNafria let his wife hold him while one of the security guards walked across the room to investigate the disturbance.

"Everything all right?" the guard asked Jody DeNafria. He was a tall thin black man in uniform. He looked directly into her eyes.

DeNafria ignored looking at the security guard and flashed his badge instead.

The guard repeated his question to Jody DeNafria. "Are you okay?"

"Yes," she said. "We're fine. There's no problem. Thank you."

The security guard took one more look at DeNafria and turned away. DeNafria was still holding his badge out and looking up at the ceiling. When he finally looked down at his wife again, DeNafria couldn't help but look beyond her and see her friend in the background. He clenched his teeth hard enough to chip one.

"Fuck!" DeNafria said. He spit the piece of chipped tooth into his hand and looked at it.

"You're all upset over nothing," his wife said.

DeNafria was seething.

"I can't have you acting this way," she said.

DeNafria felt inside his mouth with a finger for blood.

"Are you alright?" she asked.

DeNafria checked his finger for blood.

"John?"

DeNafria looked over his wife at the man he knew she was seeing. "He fuck you?" he asked her.

"Jesus Christ," she said again.

"Yes or no, Jody," DeNafria asked. "It'll make it a lot easier if you answer me."

"I'm not doing this now," she said.

"I'll take that as a yes," he said.

They looked at each other until DeNafria felt himself tearing and turned away. "Tell my son that I was here for him," he said.

Chapter 29

They met at P.G. Kings, a restaurant and bar across the street from the Empire State Building. It was a long-established staple of New York's eating and drinking world. The first thirty yards of the place was a beautiful dark oak bar along the right wall. The back room was deep and spacious with glass murals on the back wall highlighting the oak walls. The floor was green-and-white mosaic tile. For years restaurant guides have been rating the men's room at P.G. Kings the best in New York City.

Pavlik met Berra in the spacious back room between meal shifts. The tables were empty except for a few straggly drinkers. Most of the afternoon crowd at P.G. Kings were seated at the long bar. They watched a baseball game on televisions suspended from the ceiling at each end of the bar.

"You're the tough guy smacked the old man around?" Pavlik asked Larry Berra.

"I apologized to Vittorio about that," Berra said.

Pavlik glared at Berra. "And now you're afraid of getting smacked around yourself," he finally said.

"I'm afraid of getting killed," Berra said.

Pavlik lit a cigarette. "By who?" he asked.

"Jimmy Bench-Press," Berra said. "He wants to kill me."

"How do you know that?" Pavlik asked.

Berra handed Pavlik a VCR tape. "Because of this," he said.

Twenty minutes later, both men were sitting in an office in the basement of the restaurant. Pavlik was friendly with the owners at P.G. Kings. They let him use the office to view the VCR tape on a nineteen-inch television.

"It looks like your girlfriend is into porn," Pavlik said. "Do I need to watch anymore?"

"I think they're working together," Berra said.

Pavlik used the remote to stop the tape. "Working together on what?" he asked.

"Getting me to pay for the tape," Berra said. "Somebody dropped it off at the front desk where I live. I called Leanna and she told me what they wanted. She claims she was drugged when they shot this. She said Mangino fed her pills and did this without her knowledge. If you watch closely, she does look drugged. They never do a close-up of her face. Except, you know, when they're . . . They hide her face except for that."

"She tell you that?" Pavlik asked.

"It's true," Berra said. "Watch the tape again. But they want me to pay for all four copies. That's how many they claim there are, four."

Pavlik brushed lint off the jacket Berra was wearing. "They ask you to buy a bridge, too?"

"I told her I wouldn't pay them," Berra said. "I told her how could I trust her anymore, but I'm afraid if I don't pay them, they'll kill me."

"And how much do they want for this performance?"

"One hundred thousand."

"Why not a million?"

"They know I don't have it."

"They know you don't have a dime. It's your mother's money. Even we know that story."

Berra wiped sweat from his forehead. "Vittorio said he spoke to you, that you would help."

"If you fill out a formal complaint," Pavlik said. "But what do you have to complain about, aside from losing the money you loan-sharked to some old man and his girlfriend? You don't have to give them the money for the tape."

Berra was trying his best not to cry. "The old man just tried to kill me," he said.

"Huh?" Pavlik said.

"He claims somebody went to his house and mugged his wife or something," Berra continued. "Probably Jimmy Bench-Press."

"It wasn't Mangino," Pavlik said.

"Then somebody Mangino sent," Berra said. "The old man thought it was me that sent them. I didn't. I swear to fucking God I didn't. The old man, Vittorio, he came to my house and fired a gun at me. He hit the wall behind me."

Pavlik pouted and spoke sarcastically. "Nobody likes you, do they?"

"Are you going to help me or not?" Berra asked.

Pavlik shut one eye as if he was thinking about it. "Don't pay the money," he said.

"And they'll kill me," Berra said.

"They tell you that?" Pavlik said. "Because that would be extortion. Then we'd have something to work with."

"Not in so many words," Berra said.

Pavlik stalled. He rocked his head from side to side.

"What do you want me to do?" Berra finally asked.

He was inside the Tangorra house again. This time Fama had followed the old man home from the bus stop. He had waited until Tangorra was at his front door before rushing up behind him and forcing his way inside again.

Now Fama stood over Vittorio Tangorra in the dining room. The old man was tied to the chair he was sitting in. Fama had already broken the old man's nose with a hard punch in the face.

"You think you can call the cops on me?" Fama asked Tangorra. "You old prick."

"Please, go away," the old man begged. "I no call the cops again. Just a'go away."

Fama smacked Tangorra hard across the face. The old man's head whipped to the right from the force of the smack. Tears formed in his eyes.

Fama snarled as he spoke to Tangorra in their native language. "*Sono siciliano appena come voi. Come ratto sulla vostra propria gente? Come li pensate potete ottenere via con quello? A Palermo, abbiamo tagliato le linguette dei ratti. Forse dovrei tagliare la vostra linguetta, eh?*"

Fama released the blade of his stiletto. The old man's eyes opened wide with terror. Fama had just told Tangorra that in Palermo they cut out the tongues of rats, and he suggested that maybe he should do the same thing now.

"If you're lucky, nothing will happen," George Wilson said.

They were sitting on the white leather couch in Leanna's

apartment. Wilson had come there from his office. Leanna had played less than a minute of the tape for him on the VCR when Wilson took the remote from her hand and stopped the tape.

"This is kidnapping, rape, and extortion," he told her. "You could put these clowns away close to forever."

Leanna shook her head. "And the tape would become public," she said.

Wilson was going through the mini-cassette tapes she had in her purse. "Or they'll hold the tape over your head and try to squeeze Larry," Wilson said.

"Mangino said he'd give me twenty percent," Leanna said. She had been staring straight ahead. Now she looked at Wilson. "He wants to implicate me in this."

Wilson bit his lower lip. "Assume Larry pays," he said. "That'll be his problem. But don't believe that that would be the end of it. Not so long as you don't react."

Leanna shook her head again. "I can't," she said. "I can't do that to myself."

"And I can't do anything for you unless you make it official," Wilson said. "You'd have to file a complaint."

"He laughed at me," Leanna said. "That bastard laughed at me."

Wilson plugged in earphones and listened to the cassette tape in the recorder. He squinted as he made a face. He pulled the earplugs off and set the recorder down.

"Nothing," he said.

"What?" Leanna asked.

Wilson shook his head. "There's nothing on the tape," he said. "Mangino must have switched tapes."

Leanna looked up at the ceiling and closed her eyes in frustration.

"What about Larry?" Wilson asked. "How did he get a copy of the tape?"

Leanna continued to lean her head back with her eyes closed. "Mangino?" she offered without emotion. "Probably him."

Wilson touched her arm. "Leanna?"

She opened her eyes and looked at him again. "Larry said it was delivered to his building. They called him from the front desk. He called me and I told him what happened, what Mangino wanted."

Wilson was trying to maintain eye contact. "And?"

Leanna looked down again. "He said he couldn't trust me," she said. "He thinks I'm trying to rob him." Her eyes filled with tears. "They've made me the guilty party in all this."

Wilson touched the end of her chin and guided her head up. "Do you want to go to the hospital?" he asked.

"I thought that if I seduced you, that if we were involved, because you were FBI, nothing bad could really happen to me," she said. "I thought I'd be safe."

"Not without a formal complaint," Wilson said. "I tried to make you understand that."

"And now they have a tape of me with those . . . I don't even remember what happened. I don't remember how it happened. I just drank a soda and felt sleepy. That was it."

"They drugged you," Wilson said. "Which means there's still traces of what they used in your system. If we go to a hospital . . ."

"He wasn't even afraid of you," Leanna cried. "He found the card and he still wasn't afraid."

"Why don't we just go to a hospital," Wilson said. He tried to take her by the hands but she stopped him.

She half-smirked. "What for?" she asked.

"Attention," Wilson said. "You might need stitches or something. We should probably have a rape kit run. In case you change your mind later. There's nothing we can do later, if you don't go to a hospital soon."

Leanna remained rigid. "No," she said with tears streaming down her cheeks. "I can't do it."

Wilson held her hands. "Leanna?"

"No," she repeated. "I can't."

Chapter 30

While Fama pushed and shoved Spiranza Tangorra out of the bedroom, her husband worked the .25mm out of his front pants pocket. His hands were tied at his sides but he was able to rip the worn fabric of his pants pocket enough for the handle of the small caliber gun to show.

Spiranza Tangorra shrieked when Fama shoved her to the floor and told her to stay on her knees. She shook from fear. She looked to her husband but couldn't bring herself to cry.

Vittorio Tangorra looked down at his wife with tears in his eyes. He cried as he begged her to forgive him.

"Take off your rags," Fama told the old woman.

Spiranza Tangorra looked up at the man with the knife and slowly removed her nightdress.

"Yuck," Fama said. He turned to Vittorio Tangorra. "She need her teeth to give head?" he asked.

"Please," Vittorio Tangorra begged Fama.

"Fuck you," Fama told him. "Hurry up!" he yelled at the old woman.

Spiranza Tangorra was naked except for baggy undergarments. Bruises from the last time Fama had shoved her around spotted the right side of her frail body.

"Blow him," Fama yelled at the old woman. "Take his wrinkled dick out of his pants and put in your mouth."

Vittorio Tangorra closed his eyes. The old woman leaned forward and opened her husband's belt buckle. Fama looked behind him at the refrigerator and said, "Keep going," as he walked into the kitchen.

Spiranza Tangorra saw her husband motioning with his body and eyes down to his right. She looked and saw the gun jutting out of his right pants pocket. She took it in her hands. She held it with both hands and finally looked up at her husband.

"Shoot him," Vittorio Tangorra whispered.

Spiranza Tangorra closed her eyes tight.

"Not even a fucking beer in the house," Fama was saying when he came back into the dining room. "What the fuck do you people drink?"

"Shoot him!" Vittorio Tangorra yelled to his wife.

Fama's froze upon hearing the words. He looked down and saw the old woman pointing the gun at him. He turned to run back inside the kitchen when the pop of the .25mm sounded. Fama felt the sharp pain in his back as his body staggered off balance into the kitchen cabinets. He crashed hard into the stove. He reached behind him to feel for blood. Three fingers of his right hand were soaked with it. He tried to stand but his legs immediately gave out under him.

Fama felt as if the world was moving in slow motion. The pain in his back burned. His muscles seemed to act on their own. He saw himself out the door and into the street. He saw himself running down the block to the car he had parked on the avenue. He saw himself racing away in the car. Then his face touched the floor again and all he could see was the green-and-white checkered linoleum.

Fama heard a commotion in the other room and turned to see what it was.

Vittorio Tangorra appeared in the kitchen holding the gun his wife had just shot Fama with. He looked down at the gangster and spit. "*Stronzo,*" Tangorra said. "You go to hell now."

Jack Fama was still seeing himself fleeing the house as Vittorio Tangorra fired three consecutive bullets into the back of his neck and head.

Benjamin Luchessi arrived at the Canarsie pier a few minutes before Larry Berra. He was dressed in a white nylon sweat suit with purple trim. He was reading the next day's *Racing Form* under a light on the pier. He had planted his right foot on a bench under the light and turned his back to the breeze coming off Jamaica Bay.

When Larry Berra approached Luchessi, he was carrying a small black gym bag. He leaned into the breeze as he set the bag on the bench.

"What's that?" Luchessi asked.

"Fifty thousand," Berra said.

Luchessi immediately looked around himself on the pier. He spotted a beat-up van fifty yards from where they were standing and stared at it a while.

"What's it my birthday, I don't know it?" Luchessi asked.

"It's what Mangino told me to bring you," Berra said.

Luchessi made a face. He turned toward the van again and tried to spot a driver.

"I'll have the rest in two days," Berra said. "I can't do better than that."

"The rest of what?" Luchessi asked, turning his attention back at Berra. "What the fuck are you talking about?"

"The money for the tapes," Berra asked. "Leanna's tapes. The tapes of her getting fucked by two kids. The ones you made today."

Luchessi grabbed Berra by the collar. "The ones I made?" he said. He shook Berra hard, then let go. He ran his hands up and down Berra's body to check for a wire.

"You really think I'd do something like that?" Berra asked.

"Why, you any different than anybody else?" Luchessi asked. He was kneeling then. He ran his hands up the inside and outside of Berra's legs. When he was satisfied, he stood up.

"Now, what the fuck is this about?" Luchessi asked Berra again.

"Jimmy Bench-Press told me to bring this money to you," Berra said. "He said he wanted one hundred thousand but I could only get fifty tonight. I need another few days for the rest."

Luchessi took a deep breath. He looked around himself one more time and pointed at the bag. "How many days?" he finally asked Berra.

"Two," Berra said. "Three at most."

Luchessi eyeballed Berra. "Make fucking sure," he said.

Berra swallowed hard as he looked away from Luchessi's stare.

"Hey!" Luchessi said. "You hear me? Or those tapes are all over the city by the weekend."

"I'll get it," Berra said.

"Let me hear you say it," Luchessi said. "Capishe?"

"I understand," Berra said. "I'll get it. I understand."

Luchessi held his stare another moment before forcing himself to smile. "Good boy," he said. He picked up the black leather bag and pointed away from the pier. "Now get lost."

Berra frowned as he turned away from Luchessi. He walked the length of the pier to his car. He had just started the car when he heard the sirens and saw the lights. He scratched at the wire that was taped under his scrotum.

DeNafria had met Pavlik in the surveillance van on the Canarsie pier a few minutes before Benjamin Luchessi pulled into the parking lot with his daughter's Mustang. Pavlik had filled DeNafria in about the setup they were running over the telephone. Larry Berra had agreed to cooperate with them. They were going after Benjamin Luchessi.

When Benjamin Luchessi started the Mustang, the unmarked police cars immediately moved in. Luchessi backed the Mustang up as fast as he could and slammed into the back of the surveillance van. When DeNafria and Pavlik emerged from the van with their weapons drawn, Luchessi panicked and tried to scare them out of the way with the car. He was closest to hitting Pavlik when DeNafria shot Luchessi through the windshield.

Now an EMS team was working on the two bullet wounds in Luchessi's chest. Pavlik stood with DeNafria a few yards from the scene. He draped an arm around his partner's shoulders and tried to comfort him.

"You did the right thing," Pavlik said. "I was drawn and ready to fire too. You were faster than me. You did the right thing."

DeNafria nodded. "Thanks," he said.

"You're going to be alright," Pavlik said. He removed his arm from around DeNafria's shoulders and searched his jacket pocket for cigarettes.

"I don't think he meant to run you over," DeNafria said.

Pavlik immediately stood in DeNafria's face. "Yes you did think that," he said. "Yes you did or you'll be going through another fucking trial for nothing. This guy is a scumbag. He tried to run us over. Both of us. You got him before I did. That's what the fuck happened, John, and that's what the fuck you say. Alright? You hear me?"

"I guess," DeNafria said, somewhat reluctantly.

"You know," Pavlik said. "You fucking know."

DeNafria forced himself to nod again.

Chapter 31

The first thing Jimmy Mangino did after becoming a made man was get arrested. He wasn't off the cabin cruiser in the Sheepshead Bay marina more than five minutes when a dozen or so federal agents swarmed the docks.

It was late in the morning. The hookers the boat had picked up off the Arthur Kill Basin on Staten Island shaded their eyes from the bright sun. The women were herded into a police van parked at the end of the dock on Knapp Street. The underboss and captains that had presided over the ceremonies had already been picked up after they left the boat in the hooker exchange on Staten Island. Mangino and his two new Vignieri colleagues were handcuffed and placed in separate cars.

Special Agent Feller waited in Mangino's car with a camcorder. He waited until the car was moving along the Belt Parkway heading west toward the city before showing Mangino the tape made outside Eugene Tranchatta's apartment.

Mangino watched the tape and turned away from the camera. "We figure you whacked Tranchatta between your appearances on that tape," Feller said.

Mangino remained silent.

"We had the tape enhanced and lo and behold, we can make

out the handle of a .9mm Beretta. Same caliber as the bullets that killed Tranchatta and the two Korean punks in the parking lot at the Brooklyn Inn."

Mangino looked out over the Narrows.

"Aaaand," Feller said, drawing it out sarcastically. "You'll never guess how we knew about your little party last night."

Mangino let out an exaggerated yawn.

"Jack Fama," Feller said.

Mangino whipped his head around.

Feller smiled. "They make you prick your finger and do the bullshit with the picture of the saint?" he asked.

"What about Fama?" Mangino asked.

Feller was looking off in the distance, laying it on thick. "I guess he did the same thing," Feller said. "Pricking the finger, I mean. Burning the saint."

Mangino clenched his teeth.

"All that hocus-pocus," Feller continued. "They make you cross your heart and hope to die? They might as well, right? None of you guys can hold a secret anyway. Not a single one."

"Where is Fama?" Mangino asked.

"Who knows," Feller said. "Frankly, who cares? Now that we got a Vignieri Boy Scout initiation, Fama is a second rate rat."

Mangino forced a smirk. "What makes you think I'll flip?" he asked.

Feller turned the mini-television back on and nudged Mangino for his attention. "That's murder right there," he said, pointing at the small screen. "Premeditated, the way it looks on here. That's a minimum twenty-five to life. It could mean an injection to take all the pain away."

Mangino continued smirking. "You don't have anything on there," he said.

Feller slapped Mangino on the knee. "You know what?" he said. "Even if we didn't, I'll bet we could get Jack Fama to say it was a hit. To keep him from going back to Sicily, I mean. That's what gives him the creeps in the night. The thought of going back to the old country."

Mangino lost the smirk. "Fama really flipped?"

"Or maybe it was one of the other two bozos joined the Boy Scouts with you last night," Feller said.

"Now you're being a jerkoff," Mangino said.

"Really?" Feller said. "Okay. We can prove it but what the hell do we care. You, one of the other two clowns, one of the mob captain kangaroos gave out merit badges last night, one of you will do a back flip. It's the way of your world, tough guy. Sooner or later, everybody wants to play "let's make a deal." Nobody wants to do time anymore. The joint just ain't what it used to be for wiseguys. No more steak and lobster. No more red wine and all-night card games. They do another *Goodfellas* now, the movie, it'd be pretty fucking boring, the prison scenes."

Mangino tried his best to ignore the wisecracks. "And how did Fama know anything about last night?" he asked.

"He's a Vignieri by blood," Feller said. He turned toward the window and squinted from the sun. "Like I said, what's the difference? Fama, somebody else. It doesn't really matter anymore." He turned back toward Mangino. "You're the loser sitting next to me on your way to getting booked, my friend. That's the hard cold fact right now. It's all that really matters, you think about it."

"Motherfucker," Mangino said.

"Yep," Feller said. "In the meantime, you think it over. You have about twenty minutes before we reach the city. Then we take you inside Federal Plaza. Either you enter the building through the front or the back, depending on your decision. One keeps you alive and on the streets. The other maybe kills you or puts you away the next hundred years or so. You tell us what you want. Like I said, think it over." Feller glanced at his watch. "You still have nineteen minutes."

Mangino swallowed hard. He felt a headache coming on. He tried to lean his head back and close his eyes but it was too uncomfortable a position with his wrists handcuffed behind him.

Chapter 32

They sat at a round table in the back of P.G. Kings. It was after hours. The place was closed except for the four detectives and Aelish Phalen drinking and smoking at the round table. Alex Pavlik sat between his old and new partners, Dexter Greene and John DeNafria. Arlene Belzinger sat alongside Aelish Phalen with Greene to Aelish's right. She was sitting next to DeNafria but his chair was at least one full spot away. All five of them were somewhat drunk. Pavlik was inebriated.

DeNafria was holding a fresh bottle of Heineken in his right hand. He glanced at the pug, Natasha, asleep on folded linen on the floor. "I can't believe you stole Tony Pug's dog," he said.

Pavlik held up his right arm. He was holding a half-filled bottle of Souza Tequila. "Correction," he said. "Tony Pug's pug."

Dexter Greene was shaking his head. "Ain't the man annoying," he said to both DeNafria and Belzinger. "Correction. Correction this. You stole a man's dog."

Pavlik turned to Belzinger. "You see how he really is, I hope," he said. "I hope you're paying attention. The man is the relentless jealous type. It never stops. I was stuck with him for eight years, trust me."

"Aelish, what the hell are you doing with him this long anyway?" Greene asked her. "Me, I had to work with him."

"He works long hours," Aelish said. "He used to anyway."

Belzinger was giggling. She glanced up at DeNafria and saw he was looking back at her. "What about you, John?" she asked. "Did you find Alex difficult?"

Greene and DeNafria looked to each other. "Alex?"

Belzinger giggled again. "I'm trying to be polite here."

"Alex?" Greene repeated.

"He wouldn't let me call him Alex," DeNafria said. "In fact, he insisted I call him Pavlik."

"Yeah, he thinks it's more macho people know he's a big dumb Polish cop," Greene said. "He don't know they rolling they eyes soon as he tells them his name."

"They this and they that," Pavlik said. "That's what I miss the most about Dex, you know. My new prodigy, John here, he can actually speak the mother tongue. Dex is all wound up in the Ebonics thing. We's be, you's be, everybody bees free. That how it go, Dex?"

Pavlik started to laugh hysterically at his own joke.

Greene turned to Belzinger. "You see what I'm saying now? The man is a fool. Like that cripple in the opera. What was his name, the buffoon? That's what Pavlik is. A buffoon. A big one, too."

"He was trying to say *Rigoletto*," Pavlik told Belzinger. He turned to DeNafria. "Defend me, John."

DeNafria was watching Belzinger.

"Never mind her, man, she's homicide," Pavlik said.

DeNafria turned to Pavlik. "Huh? Oh, right, right. What you

say, Dex, a buffoon? That's about right, I think. That's pretty accurate."

Aelish started to clap as she laughed.

"Hey, you're supposed to be on my side," Pavlik said.

"I was while you were employed, love," Aelish said. "But you're pretty much worthless now. Until you can find yourself a movie theater to work security at or something."

Greene stood up from his chair to applaud. DeNafria followed. Belzinger and Aelish turned to each other and did a high five.

Pavlik took a swig from the Souza Tequila bottle. He waited for Greene and DeNafria to sit again.

"Shot got you there, partner," DeNafria said.

"I got that all covered," Pavlik said. "No movie theaters for me. I'm a private investigator as of Monday morning. I'm going to work for Charlie DeStefano out on Long Island. He's got work enough for me, he said. I may take a partnership."

Greene made a face. "Charlie DeStefano, the guinea, no offense John, used to sing at all those cop bachelor parties. The guy thought he was a tenor or some shit?"

"The same," Pavlik said. He took another swig from the bottle. "The man actually has opera in his blood, Dex. Somewhat the way you have rhythm in yours."

"And small dicks in yours?" Greene said.

Aelish clapped.

"Wooooooo!" the rest of them joined in.

Pavlik was trying to suppress a smile. "Now that was a very low blow," he said.

"Who is this guy?" DeNafria asked. "DeStefano. It sounds familiar but I can't place him."

"Another good cop tossed aside by the system," Pavlik said.

"More like by his partner," Greene said. "His partner was a dirty cop. He got bagged with drugs and some other stuff and immediately implicated DeStefano and a few other good cops. Jack Russo, for one. They went down in a police witch-hunt a few years back. It was up in the Bronx."

"I know of Russo," DeNafria said. "From a few people."

"The man is driving a radio car to make ends meet," Greene said. "Runs a small sheet for a local bookie, too. Nickel-and-dime sheet to pay for his kid and the lawyer he had to defend himself with."

"He was a good cop," Pavlik said seriously. "He should get in touch with DeStefano."

"Him I don't know," DeNafria said. "The name is familiar, though."

"Somebody in his family was the great tenor, DeStefano," Pavlik said. "The guy was involved with Callas, they made the famous *Tosca* recording."

"This from that class you took?" Greene asked. "Or you just making it up on the fly?" He turned to DeNafria. "He does that a lot, you know. Makes things up whenever it's convenient to his nonsense."

DeNafria was smiling at Belzinger. Greene turned to Belzinger and saw she was smiling back.

"You two think you can stop yourselves a minute here?" Greene said to them.

"Leave them be, Dex," Aelish said.

"White people," Greene said.

Pavlik spoke at Belzinger. "Don't tell me you're actually interested in this one," he said.

"I think he's cute," Belzinger said defiantly.

"He's cute?" Pavlik and Greene said together. They looked at each other.

Greene yielded to Pavlik. "I'm the one is cute," Pavlik said. He turned to Aelish. "Right, honey? Aren't I cute?"

"Not in the least," Aelish said. "I've always had it for the brutes of the world when it comes to men. No, dear, you're not cute. What you are is . . . well, you're tall. You're a tall man."

Greene was up out of his chair again giving a standing ovation. Aelish stood up and took a bow.

"You really think I'm cute?" DeNafria asked Belzinger.

"Yes, I do," Belzinger said.

"I think you're beautiful," DeNafria said.

"Thank you," Belzinger said.

"Feel free to court right in front of us," Pavlik said. "Or maybe you wanna get a room? I know the owner. They got a dining room downstairs you can throw a few linens on the floor."

DeNafria was still smiling at Belzinger. "I do think you're beautiful," he repeated.

"So ask me out, why don't you?"

DeNafria was surprised. "Would you go out with me?"

"You believe this?" Pavlik asked Greene.

"Shhhh," Greene said.

"Yes, I would," Belzinger said.

"Great," DeNafria said.

Aelish put a hand on Belzinger's back. "Good for you, love," she said.

"That's it?" Greene asked.

"What?" Belzinger asked back.

"No kiss? No hug? What, you two gonna go to the movies or something."

"And five'll get you ten, it won't be black cinema, Dex," Pavlik said.

"Drink your booze," Greene told Pavlik.

"Well, John might feel awkward to kiss right here in front of all of you," Belzinger said.

"And you?" Green asked. "You going to be my partner, you got to show some. . . ."

"Balls?" Belzinger asked.

Greene blushed. "Well, you, ah. . . ."

Belzinger looked straight into DeNafria's eyes. "I don't have a problem with it," she said.

DeNafria fidgeted with his beer.

"You making the man nervous," Greene said.

"And you're talking too much," Pavlik said. He turned to DeNafria. "Come on, partner. Show 'em what we're made of in O.C."

"You mean what you were made of," Greene said. "They booted your ass out."

Pavlik flipped Greene the finger. He clapped at DeNafria. "Go Johnny, go Johnny," he yelled.

DeNafria held up a hand. "Easy," he said. "Take it easy."

Belzinger slowly and seductively walked around the table. She took the beer from DeNafria's hand and set it on the table.

DeNafria moved both his hands up close to his chest as Belzinger sat on his lap. She turned to Greene and Pavlik and then winked at Aelish. She grabbed DeNafria by the hair and kissed him long and hard on the mouth.

DeNafria's hands shot up in the air at first. After a while, they touched the back of Belzinger's shoulders as she continued to kiss him. Eventually, he was locked in an embrace with her.

Pavlik looked at Aelish. "I wish I could get it up when I'm drunk," he said.

"So do I," Aelish said.

Greene looked to the pug on the floor and frowned. He whispered, "White people."

About the Author

CHARLIE STELLA is a writer long familiar with the street life of New York City, which figures substantially in his off-Broadway plays *Coffee Wagon, Mr. Ronnie's Confession,* and *Double or Nothing* as well as in his first novel, *Eddie's World.* He lives in New Jersey.